Broken Sky

#4

Broken Sky

#4

Chris Wooding

Cover and illustrations by Steve Kyte

AN
APPLE
PAPERBACK

SCHOLASTIC INC.
New York Toronto London Auckland Sydney
Mexico City New Delhi Hong Kong

No part of this publication may be reproduced in whole or in part, or stored in a retrieval system or transmitted in any form, or by any means, electronic, mechanical, photocopying, recording, or otherwise, without written permission of the publisher. For information regarding permission, write to Scholastic Ltd., Commonwealth House, 1–19 New Oxford Street, London WC1A 1NU, United Kingdom.

ISBN 0-439-12866-8

All rights reserved. Published by Scholastic Inc., 555 Broadway, New York, NY 10012, by arrangement with Scholastic Ltd.

SCHOLASTIC and associated logos are trademarks and/or registered trademarks of Scholastic Inc.

12 11 10 9 8 7 6 5 4 3 2 1   0 1 2 3

Printed in the U.S.A.
First Scholastic printing, November 2000

Broken Sky

(#4)

Broken Sky

JAAN

BANE

KOTH
TARAAN

1

Too Many Mirrors

The corona of Kirin Taq's dark sun was mimicked by the sea below, the rippling waves tearing the hoop of slowly writhing fire into a shivering circular smudge on the black water. The air was the temperature of a cool summer's night, tempered by a sharp breeze that sliced along the coast. But it was not summer; nor was it night, even though the world turned under a velvet-blue sky, and the glow of the sun was barely more than that of a bright moon. Kirin Taq — the dark mirror-world to the sun-washed lands of the Dominions — knew neither seasons nor the cycle of day and night. The sun was a depthless hole in the sky, outlined by its ring of lazily coiling flame, and it never moved.

Crouched along the black-sand beach, the village of Mon Tetsaa threw shimmering blobs of torchlight into the sea, a net of man-made stars that reflected the sprawling outline of the busy fishing port. It was nestled in a large inlet, where two thick arms of land reached out from the coast and formed a natural harbor. Within the sheltering embrace of the cliffs, the beaches were crowded with long, straight jetties studded with tethering-posts and torches mounted on high poles. The shallow-bottomed boats of Kirin Taq were in profusion all around, black shadows of all shapes and sizes, rocking gently against their moorings. At the harbor mouth, a double-masted ship with a long, narrow keel was slowly ploughing out to open water, almost invisible except for the bright torches along its hull and prow.

Along the waterfront, the inns never closed. Music drifted through the air, the throaty sound of a boneholler clashing with the raucous, jagged chords of a jing vaa playing a little further along. Both were accompanied by the thumping of feet and clapping of hands, different rhythms coming from different inns. The scent of frying fish and heavy spices was thick in the air, and there was sweetbread baking nearby. But for the two strangers who trod the rickety, moisture-warped planking of the waterfront, there was no time for merriment. They had an appointment to keep.

They followed the inns along the main strip, keeping the black beach and the sea beyond on their right. The girl glanced up at the inn signs as they passed; the boy kept a wary eye out from beneath his heavy hood, watching for the cold gleam of Guardsman armour. Eventually, the girl grabbed her brother's arm. "That's it," she said.

He didn't acknowledge her statement, but she knew he had heard her. They continued to walk, making their approach towards the curving, horseshoe-shaped building. In common with most Kirin architecture, it had no hard edges, and the corners were blunted. In the planking of the forecourt stood a tall pole with a banner depicting a striking symbol that furled and rippled in the biting breeze. It was a twisted pictogram, painted in dark slashes of black on a white background, with the lines seeming to curl around and behind each other in a curiously three-dimensional way.

"What's that supposed to be?" the girl asked. The only reply was a shrug. She glanced at her hooded companion, his face deep in shadow. "Chatty today, aren't we?" she observed brightly.

"I shouldn't have come with you," he said. "I stand out too much."

She blew derisively through her lips. "This is a town full of Marginals. Coastal folk. They must get all sorts through here. I bet it's so *exciting*."

The boy sighed. "Are we going in?"

"Oops, better not keep him waiting," she said, and they stepped inside.

The interior of the inn was lit warmly by the glow from a deep fire-trench that ran along the center of the floor. A triple railing of black wood kept people from falling in, except when it lunged across the trench at one of the many short bridges that spanned the fiery gap. Mirrors on the ceiling spread the light across the room. All around, wicker mats were placed for sitting, and low, teardrop-shaped tables made of a black, reflective stone stood between them.

The boy drew the hood of his cloak closer over his head. He was aware that hiding his face in such an obvious manner would draw just as much attention as if he showed it. It didn't matter. He couldn't take all their eyes bearing down on him, despite his sister's assurance that they would not notice. The hood stayed on.

"There he is," he said, squinting at someone on the far side of the fire-trench. She looked back at her brother, and gave him a reproachful glance as she saw his hood still up. Sighing to herself, she let it pass without comment. "Come on."

They stepped through the clusters of Kirins, sitting cross-legged on their mats, eating and talking in their lilting, lyrical tongue. The fine bones of the Kirin kind were roughened in the Marginals, generations of hard workers replacing elegance with strength. Their skin was a lighter shade of grey than the deep ash of the pure-breeds, and their brows were slightly wider; but the eyes were the same, cream irises on a white background, flicking this way and that as they conversed and gesticulated.

The boy closed his own eyes for a second as if in shame, as he and his sister walked across one of the short bridges that spanned the firepit. A dry, hot updraft billowed up to meet them from the bed of glowing coals beneath, racing under the hems of their cloaks and crawling up their backs. And then it was gone, and they sat down at one of the teardrop tables opposite the man they had come to meet.

"Show me the halfbreed," he said.

The boy arranged himself on the wicker mat, and then briefly slid back his hood, exposing his face. His skin was coffee-colored, a warmer shade than the Kirin grey. His nose was blocky, and his lips a little thicker than usual. But it was his eyes that gave him away; for his irises were a saffron yellow. He pulled his hood over his face again. Half Kirin and half Dominion stock. Half shadow and half light.

"I apologize," the Kirin said nervously, glancing around in case anyone had seen. "You understand I wanted to be sure. Your . . . um . . . face is proof of who you say you are."

"That's alright," the girl said. "And we know *you're* who you say you are."

"Taacqan," he said tersely, by way of introduction.

"My name is Peliqua, and this is my brother Jaan," said the girl. She was older than the other, seventeen winters by Dominion-time, with red cornrow braids that fell down her back.

"Your brother?" Taacqan queried, his eyes flicking from one to the other. Unlike Jaan, she was a purebreed Kirin.

"Half-brother," she corrected. "But it's only a term. We've always thought of ourselves as brother and sister. We just happen to have different fathers. His was from the Dominions."

Taacqan relaxed a little. Somehow he felt more comfortable talking to her, and avoided meeting her hooded companion's gaze.

"Um . . . would you like drinks?" Taacqan offered.

"It's better if we don't," Peliqua replied apologetically. "We shouldn't stay. You should come and meet the others." She looked up briefly at the mirrors on the ceiling, and frowned imperceptibly. "It's not safe here."

"It would look strange if we came in here to meet this man and didn't stay for a drink," Jaan pointed out in a low, cautious monotone.

"Of course, you're right," Peliqua said, a smile springing to her face. A moment later, her smile faded, one emotion chasing the other off her features. "One drink. And don't mention . . ." she trailed off suggestively. "We could be being watched."

"Um . . . very well," Taacqan said. "I'll get them. What will you have?"

"It doesn't matter, " Jaan said, as his sister drew breath to reply. She gave him a look of pique, as if to say: *It mattered to me!*

Taacqan nodded slightly and left. The bar had a room off the main area where drinks were mixed to order, and that was where he headed. He returned a short while later with three wooden cups of jewelberry wine, a clear, blue liquid distilled from the crystalline plants of Kirin Taq. Setting it down on their table, he seated himself and they began to act out the charade of pleasant conversation.

"That sign, out in the forecourt," Peliqua asked cheerily. "What does it mean?"

Taacqan looked around warily. He was putting on a poor display of being at ease. "That? It's for protection."

"Protection against what?"

Taacqan took a shaky swig of wine. "We're on the coast *and* on the borders of civilized society. North of here are the Unclaimed Lands. It's protection against *anything.* The Marginals are a superstitious sort."

"And you're not a Marginal?"

"No. My brother was, but not by birth; he fell in with the ships and never really got out."

"Was?" Jaan queried, surfacing from his habitual quietness for a moment.

"He died," Taacqan replied. "Actually, no, he was *taken.* By the Jachyra. See, he was a Resonant, he just wanted to stay out of the way and go where they couldn't find him but they —"

"Oh! Oh! We shouldn't be talking about *that* here," Peliqua said, flustered and waving her hands.

Taacqan stopped. Was she *really* the one he was supposed to meet? Seventeen winters or so, with such a lighthearted, scatty manner? The other one seemed more reliable, with his spare conversation . . . if he had been a little older, and if he hadn't been a halfbreed. Because after all, who could trust a halfbreed? They had Dominion blood in them.

There was a minute of silence, during which they all sipped at their drinks, the cold, sweet taste in their mouths turning to blooms of glowing heat as it slipped down to their stomachs.

"What's out there?" Peliqua chimed suddenly, making an expansive gesture to indicate that she meant the sea.

Taacqan raised an eyebrow. "Near the coast, there's good fishing. Ships are the fastest and safest way of moving heavy loads in Kirin Taq. There's a lot of money in shipping. You wouldn't know to look at them, but some of the Marginals have got a lot tucked away, where Princess Aurin's tax men can't reach it." He rubbed his knuckles uneasily. "'Course, that's just rumor," he added. "I wouldn't know anything about that."

"But what about *beyond* the coast?" Peliqua asked, fascinated.

"Deepwater," Taacqan replied gravely. "Nobody goes there. No ships ever come back. There are creatures out there the size of this port that could swallow a ship whole."

"Really," she breathed, her eyes sparkling.

"Really," he said. "Anyway . . . um . . . that brings me back to that symbol in the forecourt. The Marginals are afraid that one day the things from Deepwater might start coming closer to the coast. It'll never happen, of course; the waters are too shallow. But they have all kinds of folktales about the day when the Deepwater creatures come inland, though . . . um . . . it's not like anyone actually knows whether they even have *legs* or anything. Only a few people ever saw them and survived, and that was from a great distance. But that's what the symbol is there for. Well, that and the Koth Taraan, but they're a whole different set of dice."

"The Koth —" Peliqua began, but Jaan stopped her by laying his hand on her arm.

"Look," he said, and they followed his shadowed gaze to the doorway of the inn. Three Guardsmen stood inside the door, the fourth stepping in after them. In the glow from the fire-trench, their polished black armour was edged in red slices of light that slid over them as they moved. Carrying their long metal halberds, they began to disperse, walking purposefully between the sitting groups of Kirins on the other side of the fire pit.

"Don't worry," Taacqan said, though he sounded more like he was the one in need of reassurance. "It's just . . . um . . . a routine thing. They maintain a presence along the waterfront to discourage any —"

"It's not *that*," Peliqua said, alarmed. "It's Jaan. He's a halfbreed, remember?"

"I know," Taacqan said, and for a moment he was unable to conceal the distaste in his voice.

"I don't know if you're *aware* of this," said Jaan, suppressing his anger at Taacqan's tone, "but Princess Aurin isn't keen on Dominion-folk." He leaned closer. "Now the average person just thinks I'm a freak at first glance, but if anyone works out that I'm a halfbreed . . . what do you think's gonna happen when people start asking where the *other* half came from?"

"I don't —" Taacqan began, but Peliqua spoke over him, agitated.

"Let's just get out of here," she said. "is there a way out back?"

"They'd see us leave," Jaan said. "Just sit tight. We'll have to hope they don't look too closely."

But already, a Guardsman was crossing the fire-trench, nearing where they sat. As one, they returned to their show of conversation, talking about nothing, pretending not to notice the newcomers like the rest of the inn was doing. Taacqan was sweating, his forehead glistening with moisture, and he stuttered and stumbled over his words; but Peliqua laughed readily at what he said, and she appeared entirely at ease. Jaan was silent, his head bowed beneath his hood, occasionally sipping at his cup of jewelberry wine.

The Guardsman stopped at the table next to them, and began to speak to the people who sat there. Jaan couldn't make out the words, but he could tell by their tone that the replies were civil and curt. Nobody liked Princess Aurin's Guardsmen, but antagonizing them was a sure way to make trouble for yourself. The words exchanged, the Guardsman walked over to Taacqan's table, his tall black frame looming over them as they sat cross-legged on the floor.

"You don't look like Marginals," he stated bluntly, his voice deadened by his full-face mask. His glassy black eyepieces revealed nothing of what was beneath.

"No, we're from further south," Peliqua said, a disarming smile appearing on her face. "We're up here to visit Taacqan's brother. *He's* a Marginal. Well, not by birth; but he fell in with the ships and never really got out," she added, repeating exactly what Taacqan had told her.

Taacqan started in alarm as she blithely told the

Guardsman his real name, and he had to bite the inside of his lip to stop himself from making a sound as she went on.

"And I'm Peliqua, and this is *my* brother Jaan," she said, bubbling. "Would you like to join us for a drink?"

"No," the Guardsman replied simply, then turned the blank sheen of his eyepieces onto Jaan. "It's a little hot for such a heavy cloak," he observed.

"Oh, no, you see my brother has a . . . condition," Peliqua said.

"A condition," the Guardsman repeated skeptically. Then, shifting his halberd to his other hand, he reached down and pulled back Jaan's hood. For a moment, Jaan's face was exposed, his yellow eyes glazed and staring, his head surrounded by thick ropes of black hair with threads, beads, and ornaments sewn through them; and then he flinched away, trying to hide himself, and Peliqua cried: "Oh! Oh! See?" as she pulled his hood back over his head and got to her feet, facing the Guardsman angrily. People in the room began to turn and stare.

"He had a bad birth, that's all!" she cried. "Our mother died delivering him, and he came out deformed! Did you need to show everyone? Haven't you shamed him enough?"

"Sit *down*!" the Guardsman snapped, lashing the back of his armoured hand across her face. She collapsed with a yelp and lay on the floor, sobbing.

The room was silent. Every eye was turned on the Guardsman, including those of his companions. He shifted awkwardly, and the silence dragged into an eternity. Then he gathered himself, turned to the Guardsmen near the door and said: "There's nothing here. We'll move on."

They left, their footsteps the only sound amid the barely contained hostility in the room. The thud of the door closing behind them resounded through the inn. And then, slowly, the mutterings started, buds of sentences that soon flowered into conversation, and the burble and chatter that was the lifeblood of the inn resumed.

"Um . . . are you alright?" Taacqan asked.

"Let's just get her out of here," Jaan said grimly, helping Peliqua to her feet. She pulled her hood over her head, and they left the inn, their steps followed surreptitiously by the gazes of the other revellers.

They had walked a little way along the torchlit waterfront, the chill breeze teasing at them, when Taacqan repeated his question. Peliqua had been sobbing softly as they walked, and he was moved to concern.

"Peliqua? Are you hurt?" he asked.

At that, the sobbing changed note, and turned into soft, gleeful laughter. She threw back her hood, and her eyes were dry. There was a bruise forming on one side of her jaw, but she was smiling.

"I'm okay," she said brightly. "Just stings a little, that's all."

"Then . . . you weren't . . . ?

"Oh, no," she said. "I had to distract him. If it had crossed his mind that Jaan was a halfbreed, he'd have arrested him like they do all Dominion-folk. So I provoked him, to give him something else to think about." She felt her jaw. "Ow, but you'd better appreciate this," she said to Jaan. He didn't reply.

Taacqan glanced around, to be sure nobody was near them. The waterfront was never empty, but at the moment there were only a few figures that they could see, walking or idly driving carts of seafood pulled by pak-paks, the leathery-skinned, two-legged riding beasts of Kirin Taq. The sound of music from the inns was distant now, and they were heading into an area of warehouses and storage bays, where the hulking buildings sat quietly.

"Now can we talk about . . . um . . . why you're here?" he ventured.

15

"Parakka," Peliqua said, forgetting her bruise. "You want to join Parakka, right?"

The word meant much. Parakka was the organization of traitors that had attempted to resist King Macaan's invasion of the Dominions. They had failed in that, but had succeeded instead in establishing themselves in Kirin Taq, where Macaan's daughter Aurin held the populace in a tight and cruel grip. As their legend had grown, they had become an icon for the dissatisfied; but only a few, like Taacqan, were willing to risk execution and worse by attempting to join.

"That's right," he said. "I want to be part of Parakka. And there are a dozen or so more here who feel the same."

"And how soon can you get them?"

"Within a single cycle. But first I —"

"You want to meet the others we came with," Peliqua finished.

"My associates trust me," Taacqan said defensively. "They're putting their lives in my hands. I have to be sure."

"That's okay, we understand," Peliqua said. "You know, *we* have to be sure as well. We've been watching you for quite some time."

"I guessed you would," he admitted. "But I never saw

any sign of it. I suppose that's how it should be." Suddenly he changed the subject. "Why couldn't we talk inside? Too many ears?"

"Too many mirrors," Peliqua said.

"I don't understand," he replied.

"The Jachyra," she said. "Macaan and Aurin's secret police, They travel through mirrors. They see through them."

"Mirrors?" he said, incredulous. "But . . . I thought . . . they were invisible. That they could be anywhere. That they could pluck the thoughts out of your head."

"No, silly, that's just the rumor," she said, laughing. "Macaan started that a long time ago to keep people away from the truth."

"A . . . a *rumor*?"

"You leave a rumor long enough, give it the right soil, and it'll grow into a fact," said Jaan sagely.

They walked off the waterfront after a time, heading across a ridge of scrubland. On the other side was one of the many coves near Mon Tetsaa, a short beach of black volcanic sand hidden by the surrounding land, and invisible from the sea. On the beach, a small campfire burned without smoke, with four figures sitting around it.

Peliqua led them along a steep trail that dipped down

to the beach, treading carefully along the rutted dirt track between the tall, night-blue clumps of bladegrass. Without taking her eyes off her awkward descent, she asked over her shoulder: "Why do you want to join Parakka, Taacqan?"

Jaan winced. The way she had said it, it was too obviously a set question. They were supposed to divine the motives behind new recruits by roundabout means, not by asking them directly. Subtlety had never sat easily with his sister. Still, he was interested in Taacqan's response, if only because he thought he'd already guessed why.

"My brother was a Resonant, like I told you," he said, his words sure and unfaltering. He had thought about this a lot. "Sometimes it's like that, you know. Resonant talent doesn't run in families. Well, I'm sure you know that Princess Aurin launched a great operation some time ago to round up any Resonants in Kirin Taq. I suspect she wasn't keen on the idea of people who could flip between the Dominions and Kirin Taq at will; too difficult for her to control."

"That wasn't the whole reason," Jaan said grimly, thinking of the stories he had heard. The Resonants from both worlds that Macaan and Aurin had captured had gone to become part of Macaan's foul living machines, the Ley Boosters. It had happened during the Integration, when the King had merged the Dominions and Kirin Taq so that he could invade the former world. But he did take Taacqan's point; beings that could jump between the two parallel worlds could not easily be bound by walls or cages.

"Anyway," Taacqan continued. "He managed to stay out of the way of Princess Aurin's cull by going to sea and becoming a Marginal. I didn't like what they were doing to Resonants, but I didn't know how to change it. Then he contacted me a few months ago, and told me about something he'd heard while he was travelling." He stumbled a little on the uneven ground, and Jaan, behind him, instinctively grabbed his arm to steady him. Taacqan flinched away from the halfbreed's touch, unable to help himself. Jaan withdrew, his face unreadable beneath his hood.

"Um . . . well," he went on. "Parakka was what he was talking about. An organization that intended to end the tyranny of Macaan's family. I came up to meet him, but still I wasn't ready to risk everything for the sake of bucking the Princess's law, no matter how much I hated it."

"Is that when the Jachyra took him?" Peliqua asked, her arms out to steady herself as the decline steepened near the bottom.

"Not before he'd managed to contact you," Taacqan said. "But yes, then he was taken, And that was when I decided enough was enough. I met with the others he had talked into joining him, and then went ahead with the plan he had arranged, and . . . now here I am."

The trail dissolved into a short scramble down a bundle of weather-worn rocks, and then they hopped down on to the sand. The four figures by the campfire rose as they approached, leaving their own cloaks where they sat. Peliqua led Taacqan nervously into their presence, followed by Jaan. The faces of those who waited for them were expectant in the firelight.

"Taacqan," Peliqua said, beaming. "Meet Kia, Ryushi, Calica, and Ty."

2

The Heartbeat of the Planet

Time In Kirin Taq was marked in a curiously similar way to the Dominions, Ryushi thought, even though there were no seasons or a divide between day and night. Strange, then, that they both operated on a roughly equal twenty-two hour clock. Elani would undoubtedly put it down to her theory of balance, reflection, and connection that she used to explain the coexistence of the two worlds. It had become something of a project to her, and Ryushi found it faintly disturbing that a nine-winter child (Dominion time, of course) should be compiling information on such an abstract subject, even if she was basically just expanding on the works of the ancient philosopher Muachi. But then, she should know what she was talking about; after all, she was a Resonant, and there were not many people around today who had more experience of both worlds than she. At least, not many who hadn't already been taken by Macaan for the Ley Boosters.

Ryushi closed his hand around one of the crystalline shards of a nearby Glimmer plant and broke it off from the clump. Up here, on the side of a steep hill just on the edge of the Unclaimed Lands, they grew in profusion. He held it in front of him for a moment, watching the soft blue pulse deep inside it, winking on and off. If he watched it for long enough, it would gradually change to white, and then to yellow, then a dull green, and on through all the colors of the spectrum until it came back to blue. The whole process took around twenty-two hours. The Kirins called it a cycle, and that was how they marked their days. Of course, now he'd broken it off from its connection with the earth, its pulse would gradually fade and die over the space of a few cycles. But —

"Sometimes you are *so* deep," Calica said, sitting down next to him.

"Er . . . what?" he replied stupidly, shaken out of his reverie.

"Lost yourself again, huh?" she asked, a smile curving

her catlike cheekbones in the faint light. "What were you thinking?"

"You tell me," he said with a grin, handing her the Glimmer shard.

"Okay," she said, taking up the challenge. She weighed the object in her hand for a moment, then closed her fingers around it and shut her eyes. There was a faint, almost inaudible hum as the pale white spirit-stones that were planted in her spine began to leach energy from the ground. It rose and faded again as quickly. She opened her eyes and handed him the shard back.

The milk-white spirit-stones along Calica's spine allowed her to shape the Flow — the ley energy that formed the lifeblood of the planet — in a curious form of postcognition. She could sense, just by touching an object or being in a place, the events that had occurred in the past concerning it. Sometimes she could even divine the mind of a person by contact with an object they had handled. She had done it once with King Macaan's earring; she had done it with Ryushi many times. But it was an imprecise skill, and sometimes frustratingly vague; and she never seemed to be able to divine the things she *really* needed to know.

"Treading on Elani's ground, aren't we?" she chided, teasing. "She wouldn't be happy if she caught you musing about her work."

"It's just weird," he shrugged apologetically, turning the shard in his hand and studying it. "I mean, every single one of these things pulses in the same rhythm, and in sync. It's like the heartbeat of the planet or something."

"You've got the soul of a poet," she said spuriously. "What color is it now?"

Ryushi gave her a look. They were surrounded by clumps of the things, all pulsing a tiny light of the same color in their core. Calica blushed slightly. "Blue," she said sheepishly.

"We're supposed to make our next rendezvous with Taacqan when it's gone red, so that's . . ." he tried to calculate, and then gave up. "I hate these Glimmer things," he stated, vaguely annoyed. "You know how many innocent women and children I'd kill just to get a glimpse of the sun again? It's been a year now. A *year*! And I only know *that* 'cause Hochi keeps a calendar going back at Base Usido."

Calico sighed sympathetically, brushing her orange-gold hair back from her face, and looked out over the Unclaimed Lands. Vast leagues of forested wetlands spread out beneath them, stretching to the horizon and beyond. Enormous, bare shoulders of cold rock humped out of the sea of leaves here and there, and beneath the pale canopy of drooping, water-fat foliage there brooded treacherous marshes. No wonder it was unclaimed, she thought. Who would want it?

She turned her head to look at her companion, watching him as he toyed thoughtfully with the broken shard of the Glimmer plant. Seventeen winters now, he was, though he'd missed the last one because he'd been in Kirin Taq. In profile, she studied his small, elfin features; the slope of his nose, the outline of his chin. In the year that had passed since the Integration, that face had changed from the face of a naïve and sheltered boy into something closer to a man. The change wasn't physical; it was in the way he smiled, in the glances he threw, in every nuance of expression. His blood quills had grown longer and thicker, and now they hung about his face in short, rotund tentacles, stiffened with tree sap. The set of his shoulders was stronger, betraying a new confidence in himself that had come upon him since he had first been flung out into the world by the destruction of his home. He had changed, just like they all had; yet he was still the same. And she loved him.

Some treacherous instinct told Ryushi that her eyes

were on him, and he looked up. She cast her own gaze down, flushed, embarrassed at being caught staring. He smiled laconically to himself and looked back over the Unclaimed Lands.

"Our luck's gonna run out sometime, you know," he said distantly.

"Yeah," she replied, her cheeks still hot, and eager to distract herself with conversation. "But we've had more than our fair share. It's been a year, and Macaan and Aurin still think Parakka was wiped out during the Integration."

"It can't last," Ryushi replied. "I mean, we've been growing and growing, recruiting all over Kirin Taq. But it's not enough. And the more we recruit, the more chance of getting caught." He paused. "Once Aurin knows we're in her territory, she'll hunt every valley and every forest till she finds us."

"Ryushi, you *know* that already," Calica replied. "You've known that all the time. Why the sudden gloom?"

He tilted his head upwards, to where the deep blue-black of the sky was smeared with wispy clouds of light purple. "I dunno. Just a feeling." He absently tossed the shard of Glimmer down the hill. "Like things can't go on the way they are."

Calica frowned. "Well, if they can't, they can't," she

said. "But we've done a lot of good here, you know. The Kirins don't *want* to live under Aurin's rule, they just didn't have any way to do anything about it until now. Parakka's given a lot of people a lot of hope. And we're getting strong again. I mean, not like *before,* but —"

"It's not *enough,* though," he said, frustration in his tone. "We could be ten times as strong as this and we still couldn't square up to Aurin's army of Keriags. If we had every Kirin in the land on our side, I'd still only give us a fifty-fifty chance. It's just —"

"You've been talking to Kia, haven't you?" she interrupted gently.

He adopted an expression of exaggerated guilt. "Yeah. She worries about it a lot. She thinks Parakka isn't solving the real problem."

"How so?" Calica asked, interested.

"Well, it's just that recruiting members is fine, but that's all we seem to be doing right at the moment. We can't win by force so why try? We need another way around the problem. We've got a good network of connections now; we should concentrate on something else. It's time to devote our time to trying other solutions."

"She should put it to the Council," Calica suggested. "They'd listen to her."

"She's going to, I think," Ryushi replied.

"Your sister's a strong character," she observed, some-what reluctantly.

"She's got something against *you*, though," he said. It was bluntly put, but there was no point denying it; they both knew that while Ryushi's twin had long shed the frostiness that she had developed as a defense against her grief at her father's death, she made no secret of her dislike of Calica.

"Yeah," Calica said neutrally.

"What's worse is she won't tell me *why*," Ryushi said, digging the ground with his toe. "I mean, we've not been so close since . . . y'know . . . but it's so *unreasonable* of her."

Calica made a vague noise of agreement. She had her own theories on the subject.

The fire cracked and danced in the hollow, snapping en-thusiastically as it stripped the branches of dark wych-wood down to char. Wychwood was one of Kirin Taq's greatest natural resources; in the absence of anything like glowstones — such as were common in the Domin-ions — it provided a smokeless and long-burning fuel for fires and torches, and reduced down to almost noth-ing when it was done.

Jaan reached into the fire with a stick and poked it about a little, stirring up the already fierce blaze. Next to him, Peliqua was lying on her back, looking up at the sky. On the other side of the shallow depression in the earth, on the edge of the warm hemisphere of light, Ty sat with Kia, his arms around her waist. Since Kia and the others had rescued Ty from Os Dakar over a year ago, the two had been practically inseparable, and by now holding each other was as natural to them as breathing.

"Taacqan seemed nice," Peliqua commented suddenly, breaking the silence that had hung between them for a time.

"I think he was kinda surprised," Kia replied. "He didn't expect to be meeting Dominion-folk. Can you believe that?"

"I guess he just assumed we'd be Kirins," Ty observed.

"It wasn't *that*, it was his reaction that got me," said Kia. "I should be used to it by now, I suppose, but it still catches me once in a while. Y'know, how he got that *what have I let myself in for?* expression. And why? Just 'cause our skin is pink and we've got colored irises. Where's the sense?"

"But his brother was a Resonant; he said so," Peliqua

29

protested, raising herself up on her elbows and looking across at Kia. The Dominion girl was slim, tall, and slightly gangly, with dark red hair in a ponytail and shockingly green eyes. "He *must* have seen Dominion-folk before."

"Old prejudices run deep, and we get scared of people that are different," Kia said. She tilted her head back so she was looking up at Ty. "Remember what Hochi was like with Tochaa?"

"Uh-huh," he said. "Besides, dear Princess Aurin has spent enough time stirring up anti-Dominion sentiment to make our job harder than it already is. She's got the whole of Kirin Taq believing that anyone without grey skin is an outlander pirate from across Deepwater, come to kill their womenfolk and destroy their way of life from within, and Macaan's done the same with the Dominions and white irises."

"Sweet girl," Kia commented. Ty made a noise of sarcastic agreement. "Using our own ignorance about what's beyond the sea to keep us apart."

"You think he'll still turn up for the second rendezvous?" Peliqua said, sounding worried. "Oh, I hope he will! We have to meet the rest of the people who want to join."

"If he doesn't, we're better off without him," Ty replied.

"We have to rely on people working *together* against Macaan — Kirin *or* Dominion-born. Parakka won't work if none of us trust each other."

"That's a manifesto if ever I heard one. You're sounding more like me every day," Kia grinned, nudging him in the chest with the back of her head.

"Can I help it if my girlfriend thinks she has a monopoly on politics in this relationship? Getting on the Council has made you too full of yourself."

"You're only jealous," she teased.

Kia had sat on the Parakka Council ever since the Integration, when she had been instrumental in the assault on the Ley Warren near Tusami City. That her suicidal bravery had owed more to blind hatred of Macaan's forces than tactical brilliance didn't matter; the troops had needed something to rally around after their crushing losses in the battle, and she had been it.

Ryushi and Ty, to a lesser extent, had also been hailed as heroes; but the death of the much-respected Otomo — for which some blamed Ty — had cast a shadow on his sacrifice, and Ryushi's discovery of the Ley Booster was seen by some as more lucky chance than anything else. And while Ryushi and Ty were uncomfortable with the attention, Kia had seemed to glory in it.

When the Council reformed after the Integration, casualties had left several posts to be filled. In the midst of the acclaim, the Council could scarcely fail to offer one to Kia, and Calica had advocated that she be appointed, despite the differences between them. Since then, she had been actively involved in the politics of Parakka, and had something of a reputation as an outspoken voice in debates.

Ty, on the other hand, had retreated from public view as much as possible, preferring to keep himself to himself. While Kia had bounced back quickly from the Integration — when she had drained herself to near-death by expending her power beyond its limits — Ty had spent a lengthy period in convalescence, recovering from the wounds sustained in the crash that had killed Otomo. It had given him a taste for peace, after his hectic months as a prisoner on Os Dakar. The skin-dyed tribal colors that he had obtained there had faded over time, his wild black hair had grown back to some extent, and now he looked more like the boy Kia had left behind at Osaka Stud, so long ago. But he had not lost the lean muscle that the hardships of Os Dakar had left on him; nor the haunted look in his eyes, nor the terrible guilt at the atrocities he had committed there.

"I'm bored," Peliqua declared after a few moments,

slumping back down to the ground again. Jaan shifted his weight next to her with a rustle. It was the most noise he'd made for an hour or more. "Well, aren't you?" she prompted him, as if his small movement had brought him suddenly back into the realm of conversation.

"I don't *get* bored," he replied.

"I do," she said, as if he didn't already know that. "So let's do something. What about you, Kia? Ty?"

Kia shuffled her shoulders comfortably within the circle of Ty's arms. "I'm just fine here," she said lazily.

Seeing that she was going to get nowhere with those two, Peliqua focused her efforts on her brother again. "Come on, Jaan. There's still three-quarters of a cycle before we have to meet Taacqan. Let's *do* something."

"Like what?" Jaan sighed.

"Let's explore," she said.

"Peliqua, you're such a kid. What's the point?"

"Because it's fun!"

"It's *not* fun, it's dangerous. We're right on the edge of the Unclaimed Lands."

"I'll protect you, little brother," she replied with a grin.

"I don't want protection, I want you to leave me alone," he said.

"No you don't," she declared decisively, getting up and dragging him up by the hand. "Come on! Let's get away from these two for a while." She winked at Kia and led her limply protesting brother away from the fire.

"What is *up* with you today?" Peliqua asked. "You've been in a mood ever since we went to Mon Tetsaa."

Jaan waved a hanging vine aside with an expression of irritation. He might have known his annoyingly mercurial sister would drag him straight into the Unclaimed Lands. Her unquenchable sense of adventure was fine at times, but at moments like this it grated on his nerves. And now they had headed into the wetlands, the ground underfoot becoming alternately squelchy and waterlogged or dry and bristly.

"Well?" she prompted when he didn't answer.

"What did you actually hope to see out here?" he asked, deflecting her question.

"I want to climb that big rock," she enthused. "You know, the nearest one that we saw above the treeline."

Jaan squeezed his eyes shut and pinched the bridge of his nose with his fingers. "That must have been a mile in from the border," he said, praying that she would reconsider.

"Too late to turn back now!" she bubbled happily.

"That's what I thought you'd say," he muttered.

They forged onward, mostly in silence until Peliqua took to talking to herself after Jaan proved unresponsive. This was doubly annoying to him, for he now had a running commentary of everything his inquisitive sister observed, punctuated by little asides to herself about how boring and dull her brother was. As they walked, the going became worse, and they sometimes had to backtrack or detour around small bogs and sections where the dark, brackish water came up above boot-level. The trees and foliage began to take on an oppressive quality, their tubular leaves drooping low and brushing their shoulders and heads occasionally. Jaan was no longer sure that his sister actually knew where she was going, but he followed anyway, murmuring slanders under his breath.

That was when Peliqua stopped, holding out a sleek, grey-skinned arm to warn him to do the same. He was immediately on the alert, his saffron eyes scanning his surroundings. At first, he could not see what had alarmed his sister; there seemed to be no pressing danger, and there was no sound but the distant, plaintive cries of marsh-birds and the stirring of the leaves.

Then he saw.

He had probably been looking right at them and not

known what they were. They looked like boulders, hunching out of the wet undergrowth; and they were some distance away, obscured by trees and tall grasses. But now that Peliqua pointed them out, he looked hard at them. His mother's blood had given him the Kirin low-light vision, evolved through generations under an eclipsed sun; but even so, he found it difficult to discern any detail there. If he was being logical, there would be no reason to be suspicious of the hulking, immobile shapes nearby. Except that they were suddenly surrounded by them, and they hadn't been before.

The boulders had moved.

"Er . . . *this* isn't good," Peliqua said in a small voice.

Jaan groaned. "This is the point where we start regretting the fact that we didn't get to ask Taacqan about the Koth Taraan," he observed dryly.

"Koth Taraan?" Peliqua repeated, breathless with wonder. "Is that what they are?"

"*I* don't know! It's just a best guess!" Jaan replied, exasperated. His gaze flicked from one blocky shape to another; but they were too far away to make out anything beyond their shadowy outlines, and then only in glimpses between the foliage. He glanced back at Peliqua. "Still want to climb that rock?"

"No," she replied. "Uh-uh. In fact, I'm kinda thinking how nice that campfire was."

"Yeah, that's what I was thinking too," he said. "Why don't we just turn around and go back there?"

"That's a good idea," Peliqua agreed. "We could . . . *Oh*!"

Her short gasp of surprise was brought on by the sight of one of the boulder shapes suddenly moving, raising itself a little and then lumbering a few meters before stopping and settling again. In that space of time, she saw that, whatever they were, they were big. At least half her height again, and perhaps more. She had thought she would be able to make out more detail as it stirred, but the poor visibility foiled her. In moments, all was still again.

"Wasn't that the way we came?" Jaan asked slowly, nodding towards the space that the shape had vacated.

"I think so," Peliqua said.

"Think they're trying to tell us something?"

"Uh-huh."

Jaan ran his hands over the spring-loaded dagnas concealed in his sleeves. They were two-foot long, serrated blades hidden inside light wooden tubes on his forearms that could be unsheathed by knocking the tubes together hard. Their presence reassured him a little. "Come on, then," he said, and they began to walk slowly back towards the border.

The boulder-shapes lumbered aside further as they warily made their way through the gap in the surrounding creatures. Always they were just too far away to be seen in detail, displaying a surprising ability at hiding for such large-framed things. But they appeared to be keeping their distance, and that was what was important. The two trespassers were allowed to leave unharmed; and though Peliqua kept catching glimpses of something following them all the way back, she could not be absolutely certain that it was not just her imagination.

3

No One Left to Tell

Kia drew the Glimmer shard from her belt and looked at it. The pulse at its core flashed a weak browny-red. She'd had this shard for too long; it would soon be time to get another.

"Are we on time?" Ryushi asked, standing next to her.

"I'm not sure. It's so hard to be exact with these things," she replied.

Their meeting-point with Taacqan was a sheltered spot underneath a rocky bluff that hung over their heads. They were surrounded by a sparse smattering of many-armed wychwood trees, their circular blue leaves layered like scales along their limbs. The dark sun brooded in the narrow slash of sky between the treetops and the lip of the stone overhang, watching them.

"I don't like this," Ryushi commented.

"He's not even late yet," Calica said, from where she leaned against the rock wall behind them, turning her katana in the dim light and examining its edge. "You're just having a paranoid day." Calica still hadn't gotten out of the Dominion habit of referring to day and night; in fact, she maintained it on purpose, as if reluctant to forsake the ways of her homeland.

"We could have chosen a better place than this," Jaan said darkly. "It's well-hidden enough, but it'd be perfect if they decided to ambush us."

"You kidding?" Calica said. She tapped Ryushi on the arm with the flat of her blade. "Our little supernova here could clear the forest for half a mile in any direction if it came to a fight. Anyway, these people are sailors and fishermen, not warriors."

"You sound very confident, Calica," Peliqua said.

"Call it intuition," she replied slyly, "but I've got a feeling Taacqan is going to turn up real soon. Alone. And he's picked up a bit of a cold since last time we saw him."

Nobody argued with her; her spirit stones worked both ways, past *and* future, and she had a disconcerting habit of predicting things that were about to occur. This time was no exception; she had barely finished her sentence before they heard the sound of branches being pushed aside and the soft pad of footsteps on the turf. A few moments later, Taacqan appeared, sneezing explosively as he arrived.

"My apologies," he said. "I've picked up —"

"— *a bit of a cold since last time we saw you,*" Peliqua and Ryushi chorused, grinning. Calica shrugged in the background. "Lucky guess," she said, and went back to the nonchalant examination of her blade.

Taacqan frowned, aware that there was some joke going on that he didn't understand, but he decided it wasn't worth pursuing and said: "Are you all ready? The others are waiting nearby."

"Lead us, then," Kia said, pulling her bo staff up from where she had been leaning on it and casting a disparaging glance at Calica.

South of the border of the Unclaimed Lands, the wetland foliage changed to forests of wychwood and haaka, which petered out as they reached the rocky shores and cliffs of the coast around Mon Tetsaa. It was through these forests that Taacqan took them, avoiding the open land in case they should be spotted by the King's Riders on wyvern-back. As a rule, the Riders did not come this far north, tending to stay in the more populous provinces inland, but Taacqan was nervous enough as it was and was in no mood to take chances.

"What happens when you've met the others?" Taacqan asked suddenly, looking at Kia.

"Well, once they've gotten over the fact that we're Dominion-born —" Kia began, but Taacqan interrupted with: "Oh, I told them that already."

"How did they take it?"

"Two dropped out. They said they wouldn't trust their lives to Dominion-folk. The rest are . . . um . . . wary, but they still want to join. They'll come around more fully when they've had time to think. It was just a bit of a shock. I mean, first the halfbreed and now you four . . ."

"We can't pick and choose our members, Taacqan," Kia said, a little sternly. "All that's necessary is the will to resist the tyranny you live under. Anything else is purely cosmetic."

Taacqan was silent for a time, leading them through the trees without ever seeming to need to check where he was, sniffing occasionally because his nose was running. Then, at last, he spoke: "We want to learn more," he said slowly. "*I* want to learn more, be of use to you. Against Aurin."

"Then you're welcome," Kia replied. "And if your friends feel the same, we'll take it from there. What you can do depends on your individual skills. Some might be of use to us staying here, being our eyes among the

Marginals. We might need others at one of our sanctuaries. It depends."

The trees began to thin out now, dissolving into the jagged rocks, coves, and inlets of the coast. The ground was covered in scrub and shale, and their footsteps changed from thuds to crunches as they made their way down to another cove, this one even smaller and more well-hidden than the one they had first met in. Mon Tetsaa was a distant clump of lights to the north, just visible below the horizon. Here, all was silent but for the susurrant hiss of the waves and the fitful sighs of the wind.

"What are the Koth Taraan?" Kia said suddenly, as if the question had just occurred to her.

"Um . . . why do you ask?" came Taacqan's puzzled reply.

"Well, Peliqua and Jaan said you mentioned them earlier, when you first met," she said, pretending casually to scrutinize the end of her bo staff. "And last night, they went over into the Unclaimed Lands and came across something that they think —"

"They went into the Unclaimed Lands? Why?" Taacqan asked, suddenly distressed. Kia's interest was piqued; the Koth Taraan seemed to be something of an important subject to him.

"It doesn't really matter why; the point is, they did. *Do* you know anything about them?"

"Everyone in Mon Tetsaa knows about the Koth Taraan," Taacqan said. "And the first thing they learn is that they are a *very* territorial people."

"People?" Kia queried.

"Creatures," he corrected himself. "I'm sorry, I . . . um . . . used to come up here and study them. I'd live in my brother's house while he was at sea. I suppose I've spent so much time at it, it's difficult not to think of them as people. But they're not; they're mindless, violent things. Your friends were very lucky, if they got off the Unclaimed Lands alive."

"Are we talking about the same thing here? Peliqua said they looked sorta like boulders from a distance."

Taacqan made a thoughtful face. "Yes, I suppose it would have been them, anyway. There's nothing else that lives this close to the borders that is anywhere near their size. The Koth Taraan wiped them all out. You know, a group of Guardsmen and settlers and so on went in there once; the Princess wanted to expand northward, and they were testing out the territory. They never came back, and a few days later the Koth Taraan attacked Mon Tetsaa. That was about a year ago now. Like I say . . . um . . . terrible, hostile things. Mindless."

"That doesn't *sound* mindless," Kia said. "It sounds like revenge. Warning you to stay off their land."

"Oh, no, it was a rampage. They were angry. All animals get angry if you encroach on their territory."

The descent to the cove was, if anything, even rougher than the last one. The rocks slanted sharply down towards the beach, and water runoff from the higher ground had carved shallow trenches into the stone that made the footing precarious. There was no campfire here, but Jaan and Peliqua, with their keener vision, could make out the group of waiting figures on the black sand below. Eventually, the Parakkans touched down on the beach and strode across towards Taacqan's companions. One of the figures broke away from the main group to meet them. He was unusually stocky for a Kirin, with a close-cut beard of dark blue and heavy brows above his striking white eyes.

"Taacqan," he said gruffly. "These are the Parakkans?"

Taacqan introduced them each in turn, ending with the newcomer, whose name was Aran. "I didn't think you were coming," Taacqan said to his companion. "I hoped my message had reached you."

"Not before time, either," Aran replied. "A day later and I would have been on my way south again, down the coast." He paused. "I'm sorry for your brother,

Taacqan: I heard you put up a good fight before they dragged him away. How did you —"

"There'll be time for that later," Taacqan said. "For now, we have to hurry. This is a treasonous business we're on, and if we're caught . . ." he trailed off suggestively.

The other nodded. "Come, then," he said to Kia. "We must meet —"

He was cut short by a scream, tearing suddenly from the throat of one of the women in the group behind him. He whirled, a blade flashing free from his heavy belt; Kia's bo staff snapped into a ready stance; Ryushi's hand was on his sword. For a heart-stopping second, none of them could see the danger; and that sensation was perhaps worse than when their eyes finally fell on what the woman was looking at.

Rising out of the beach, sloughing black sand in a cascade from its narrow shoulders and thin back, was a Jachyra. It was a terrifying scarecrow of a figure, its unnaturally long arms and emaciated legs buried under a motley of belts and rags, sections of its body and face meshed with a dull metal so it was impossible to tell how much of it was flesh and how much was not. The feeble glow of the dark sun glimmered on the lenses of its eyes, one of them telescoping and retracting with a high-pitched whirr as it turned its head to focus on each of the traitors on the beach, settling finally on . . .

+++ TAACQAN! +++ it howled, its voice shrill with feedback and crackling with an undercurrent of static.

And then the others broke cover, and suddenly the beach seemed alive, the spindly monstrosities that were King Macaan's secret police rising like corpses from their sandy graves on all sides.

"Ambush!" Ty yelled, swinging his hooking-flail free from his belt. It was one of his mementos from his time as a prisoner in Os Dakar, and the only weapon he had really learned how to use; three weighted balls on the end of three chains, connected at the junction where he held them, and each ball with a vicious edged fin of metal jutting out from its smooth surface.

Ryushi's sword and Calica's katana scraped free of their scabbards together. "I *knew* this one was gonna go wrong," Ryushi said to himself. Taacqan was wide-eyed in terror, his attention fixed on the creature that was loping across the sand towards him, screaming his name, the sound half-voice and half-mechanism.

"What's this about?" Kia shouted, shaking him roughly by the shoulder. "Did you do this?"

"I didn't betray you!" Taacqan cried, his voice thin with fear. "I didn't!"

"Well *someone* did," she grated, releasing him and gripping her bo staff instead.

And now the screaming really began in earnest, for the first of the Jachyra had reached the group of Kirins nearby, and with a *shrik* its finger-claws slid out as one of the men ran at it with a shortblade, hoping to defend the others. But as Calica had observed, these people were not warriors. A clumsy swipe at the creature's head was easily ducked, and it raked its metal nails across the man's exposed belly as it passed without even breaking stride, dragging a spume of steaming blood with it. Unnoticed behind his killer, the man dropped shakily to his knees, his hands on his stomach, and slumped face-down into the sand.

"Run!" Ryushi shouted at the other Marginals that were assembled; but they were surrounded, penned in like sheep, and each panicked attempt to disperse only brought them face to mummified face with one of the advancing Jachyra.

"Help them!" Aran bellowed to the Parakkans, but his eyes told them that he knew it was useless. The Jachyra descended on their hapless victims without mercy, and the shrieks and howls of the would-be recruits shredded the air as the creatures set about them in a murderous fury.

It was only because Aran had met the Parakkans halfway between the main group and the edge of the cove that they had been spared the first assault; but several Jachyra had headed for them instead of the Marginals, and they were almost upon them now, with the others that had participated in the slaughter coming fast behind.

"Get out of here! Fall back!" Calica cried, her katana held before her, ready to meet the enemy. "We can't fight them!"

"I really think we *can*," Kia said blandly at her shoulder, and threw out her arms, fingers splayed. The sandy ground before her feet bulged upwards and then tore away from her towards the more distant group of Jachyra, as if some vast subterranean mole were burrowing just beneath the surface of the beach. A moment before it reached them, the bulge exploded in a stinging fountain, and something vast reared out of the earth with a roar, a huge shadow in the sandstorm. The Jachyra balked and hesitated, their lenses whirring in an attempt to see the nature of their opponent; but an immense fist smashed out of the cascade of black sand, pulverizing one of them into the ground with a sickening cracking of bones and tearing of metal.

And then the sand cleared, and they could see. Kia

49

had created a golem out of the beach, a huge, mindless shape in a vague approximation of humanoid form. Sand poured from its arms and down its body, shaking off in great curtains whenever it moved; but Kia was constantly renewing it, replenishing its body as it diminished itself. It opened the great, ragged gash that was its mouth and then, with a bellow, it attacked.

"Kia! We've got to get out of here!" Calica cried. "They'll overrun us!"

But if Kia was hearing her, she wasn't answering. Her hatred of Macaan's forces had ceased to be the controlling force in her life over the last year, but in the heat of combat she found that it still burned just as brightly, and she wasn't going to let these abominations live to massacre any more innocents.

"Ty!" Calica shouted. "Look after Kia!"

Ty nodded, his weapon still held ready. Calica outranked them all, being a former leader of the Tusami City chapter of Parakka, and they knew what a tactician she was. In battle, they bowed to her greater experience. At the same moment, those Jachyra that were not occupied with the golem reached them, led by the creature that was howling Taacqan's name, and the battle was joined.

Jaan and Peliqua leaped as one to meet the attack.

Jaan clashed his forearms together, and the blades of his dagnas snapped out with a metallic scrape; Peliqua pulled free the manriki-gusari that was wrapped around her waist. It was a long, thin chain with a heavy diamond-shaped weight at each end. Still in the air, she struck out with it, hoping to entangle the closest Jachyra; the blades of Jaan's dagnas were with her, a twin strike lashing out that would have beheaded the creature had it hit. But it *didn't* hit, because the Kirins had never fought the Jachyra before, and they were completely unprepared for the inhuman speed of their opponents. Still screaming Taacqan's name, the creature dodged their double-attack without even slowing, and rushed past them as if they were not even there. A moment later, the creature's companions joined the fray, and the Parakkans found themselves in a desperate fight for their lives.

The beach had become a battleground. Nearer the lapping edge of the water, Kia's golem fought with the Jachyra, pitching its huge strength against their far superior reactions. They darted around it as it swung at them, slashing at its legs with their finger-blades. But their attacks did no good against the black sand that was the golem's flesh; its wounds closed as fast as they could make them. Kia was keeping them occupied, preventing them from joining their companions; and occasionally, when one of the Jachyra was careless enough to allow itself to be caught, she had the pleasure of tearing it limb from limb.

Close by, the dark sun looked over the still bodies of those that the Jachyra had slain, lying in a rough heap on the blood-soaked sand.

"Help me!" Taacqan shrieked, as he was pitched off his feet and thrown hard to the sand. Aran ran to his defense, his sword upraised, but the creature that loomed over Taacqan lashed out behind itself without even looking, and opened his throat with its cruelly hooked fingers. He slumped, gurgling, to the sand, while the Jachyra crouched over the prone form of Taacqan.

"Help me!" he screamed again, but no one could. They were barely holding the creatures off as it was; nobody could afford to let down his guard for even a split-second.

+++ You left me, Taacqan +++ the creature buzzed, its patchwork face scarcely an inch from his, one claw held under his chin.

"Wh-what?" he breathed, his voice trembling so much that the word was barely recognizable.

+++ You ran. You saved yourself. You let them take

me, Taacqan +++ The creature leaned in closer until the metal grille of its mouth was touching Taacqan's lips, and he tasted oil. +++ **How could you do that to your brother? +++**

Taacqan's white Kirin eyes widened in horror as the Jachyra leaned back a little, allowing him to see its ragged body, the mummified fusion of metal and flesh that was its face. A short whistle of feedback escaped its mouth, and then it spoke again, a whisper that was mangled by the mechanism that was its voice. +++ **Look what they *did* to me +++**

"You're not *him*!" Taacqan screamed, suddenly thrashing under the creature, trying to escape from the horror that held him pinned.

+++ **Brother +++** it said, the word coming out like a curse. Keeping him held down with one hand, it studied the other one, flexing the dull metal of its fingers before the lenses of its eyes. +++ **You don't seem happy to see me back +++**

"*You're not my brother!*" Taacqan spat in the creature's face.

+++ **Not your brother? +++** came the mock-surprised response. +++ **But I remember so well the time when you broke your arm falling from a pakpak, down**

by the tree near Mother's favorite market +++ The Jachyra leaned close again. **+++ I pushed you, don't you recall? +++**

Taacqan's breath was locked in his throat, a vein jumping beneath the grey skin of his temple.

+++ I see that you do +++ it said, and then, holding Taacqan's jaw with one hand, buried its claws in his belly.

Ryushi grunted as his sword bit hard into the leg of a Jachyra, coming free in a rill of greenish fluid. He threw his head back as a clawed hand flashed out of nowhere and narrowly missed his cheek; the creature's follow-up strike was intercepted by Calica's katana. Peliqua's manriki-gusari worked alongside Jaan's dagnas, spinning and flashing through the air, whirling around her body, entangling and parrying while her brother struck out with his blades. Ty's hands were also full, his hooking-flail lashing about him as he fought to defend Kia, who was concentrating too hard on maintaining her golem to fight. They were trying to retreat out of the cove, back up the rocky trail to higher ground; but the Jachyra were so *fast,* it was impossible to concentrate on anything beyond the job of staying alive. Sweat sheened their faces as they blocked and leaped and ducked; the air seemed full of the slashing claws of their enemies.

And sooner or later, Kia was going to tire, and the golem would crumble, and they would be overwhelmed by the reinforcements on the other side of the beach.

"Ryushi!" Calica said through clenched teeth. "Stop holding back! We're losing here!"

Ryushi half-turned his head at her comment, and one of the Jachrya got a quick swipe at him, the tips of its nails grazing the edge of his throat and drawing a little blood there.

"Okay," he grated, swinging up his sword to fend off the next blow. "Fun's over."

The Flow swelled up inside him with a feverish eagerness, his spirit-stones drawing power from the ley lines that ran invisibly beneath the earth, storing it, regulating it . . . and then releasing it. He thrust out his hand, a cry of exultation escaping his lips, and a shock-wave of energy ripped through his body and along his arm, a translucent ripple of force that smashed into the Jachyra directly in front of him and annihilated it. He swung the torrent of energy towards the other Jachyra that assaulted them, blasting them apart like leaf-piles in a gale, their mechanical screams drowned in the roar of energy that poured through his body. Those who were not hit by the first blast tried to run. Some made it away, some didn't; but by the time Ryushi managed to rein himself in, the beach was a charnel house.

All was silence in the aftermath. Ryushi stumbled weakly, his legs beginning to give, but Calica bore him up. In the dim light, the glistening lenses of the distant Jachyra watched them warily. Even those that had been fighting Kia's golem had retreated to a safe distance, and were silent.

"Taacqan!" Ty suddenly exclaimed, and he ran to where a dark shape lay on the sand, its hand raised feebly. He knelt down next to the wounded Kirin, but one look at the horrendous gash in his stomach told him that there was nothing he could do. Taacqan looked up at him, struggling to speak, and Ty took the dying man's hand as he breathed his final words.

"I . . . was a coward," he said, laboring for the strength to form his words. "I didn't try to save my . . . my brother. I ran . . . and left him to die. I lied to the others about what . . . what I had done. Tell them!"

Ty's gaze was full of pity. "There's no one left to tell."

Taacqan gripped his hand hard. "The Jachyra . . . it was my brother . . . he knew things . . . only we knew . . ." he coughed, and there was a rattle from deep in his throat. "It . . . was . . . him . . ." Then suddenly, his eyes went wide, as if in alarm, remembering something he had to say before his essence finally left him. He clutched Ty's shirt front desperately with his free hand. "The Koth Taraan . . . and the Keriags . . . they . . . can . . ." he breathed, and then his eyes closed, and he died. The Jachyra that he had spoken of was nowhere to be seen, having retreated with its companions and cloaked itself in shadow.

For a moment, nobody moved. The Jachyra were keeping a safe distance, now with a healthy respect for Ryushi. The golem had stilled, and was crumbling away, its arms and legs running in cascades to join the beach again.

"Back off and let's leave," Calica said. She didn't need to add why. Ryushi wouldn't be able to pull off another burst of energy for quite some time. He had been holding back because he knew he would drain himself to exhaustion if he cut loose; and if the Jachyra sensed that, they would attack again with redoubled fury, and Parakka would have another helpless fighter to defend.

In the year since the Integration, Ryushi's ability to control his enormous power had improved slightly, but not much. It was still an uncontrollable beast that, once released, would have to be manhandled back into captivity before it burned him out. He'd bluffed a Jachyra before, in the Ley Warren near Tusami City, into believing he had a greater mastery of his power than he really did. Calica was gambling that it would work again. All evidence so far had shown the Jachyra to be essentially cowardly creatures, sneak-attackers and assassins who generally only fought when they knew they would win. Ryushi had given them something to think about now, and they were not keen for another taste.

And so, slowly, with their eyes never leaving the scarecrow silhouettes of their enemies, the Parakkans began to climb the rocky trail up the cove to the high ground, leaving their dead behind them, the scent of blood rising from the beach and mingling with the sharp salt tang of the sea.

The Jachyra watched them go, motionless. None of them made any move to pursue.

For a time, there was only the sound of the sea.

And then, without a signal or a word, the Jachyra turned as one and descended on the one who had killed Taacqan, and tore it apart.

4

Cold Gem Lying

The mainland of Kirin Taq was a webwork of provinces and their boundaries. The independence of the thanes — the rulers of each province — had been taken when King Macaan took control of Kirin Taq, turning those thanes that he did not execute outright from politically powerful figures into little more than caretakers for his land. Unlike in the Dominions, where Macaan had destroyed the thane system entirely, he allowed a diluted version of it to exist in Kirin Taq, to help watch over the land while his daughter grew and his attention was on the conquest of the other world.

Since Macaan had taken the throne in Kirin Taq, the provinces had remained strictly in order, with the family lines of the existing thanes gradually being replaced by

Macaan's favorites. His influence stretched from the Unclaimed Lands in the north to the Iron Coast, far to the south; and through all the generations his family had ruled from the same seat of power. Standing at the nexus of six provinces, the hub of Kirin Taq, was the royal palace, Fane Aracq.

It stood atop a high hill, honeycombed with roads that led away to the surrounding lands. It was a masterpiece of Kirin architecture, a construction of soaring spires and parapets that displayed no sharp edges at all. Made entirely of creamstone, it looked as if it had been carved from cloud. Standing white and ethereal in the twilight, it had no regular shape, no symmetry at all in its construction: high walkways spanned gaping drops between towers; tiny domes like bubbles nestled at their bases in clusters; blunt needles of stone bristled out in sprays, fulfilling no obvious purpose except to add to the beautiful chaos of the palace. It was a creation like no other had been before or likely would be again, and it was the home of Princess Aurin, ruler of Kirin Taq.

She stood at one of the oval wind-holes of her chambers, looking out over the land beneath her. The distant torches of a city; the beautiful blue-green fields; the banks of crystalline flowers at the edge of a river so clear that the water could only be seen by the reflection it threw of the black sun's light. All of it was hers, given to her by her father. It meant less than nothing to her. It had taken no effort on her part to attain; it had been given half out of necessity and half out of guilt. Her father had needed to leave the land in safe hands, and she was his only bloodline since the death of the Queen, long ago. And it was his way of trying to make up for her childhood, the latest of his many gifts to her, as if any material possession, even one as grand as this, could make her love him as she had her mother.

She turned away from the window. Her chambers were lit by the rare white glowstones, imported from the Dominions, that sat in brackets around the curved walls. A low, smooth table rose out of the floor, carved from the very stuff of the room itself, and was surrounded by ornately patterned wicker mats and cushions. Fragile ornaments in shades of blue sat on the wide sills of the glassless wind-holes. A huge mirror formed part of one wall, its wrought-iron frame sending writhing tentacles sewing in and out of the creamstone, meshing it to its setting. It was an exact copy of another one, a world and half a second away, in her father's sanctum in the Dominions.

For a time, she studied her own reflection. The young woman who looked back at her was strikingly beautiful.

Tall and willowy, she wore an elegant white dress trimmed in turquoise, and long, tight-fitting gloves of the same color. Her hair, in sharp contrast, was the darkest black, worn in two loose plaits at the side that coiled around to meet the rest of the silken fall in a clasp. The only jewellery she wore was a triplet of turquoise stones, a larger one flanked by two smaller ones, linked by a pair of thin silver chains around her neck. The necklace was as much a part of her as the curved lines of her eyes or the sleek bow of her shoulders. She never took it off. She couldn't. Her life depended on it.

A subtle change in the ambient pressure of the air warned her that a visitor was imminent. She took a small step back from the mirror and waited. A few moments later, a ragged, filthy claw breached the reflective surface as if breaking through a film of water — though there were no ripples as it came — and the hunched and ragged form of Tatterdemalion, Chief of the Jachyra, stepped through into the chamber.

+++ **My lady** +++ he said, dropping to one knee before her and bowing.

"You don't have to do that, Tatterdemalion," she said. "I think we have gone beyond the need for ceremony between us, yes?"

+++ **As you wish** +++ the Jachyra said, rising to his

usual bent, slouching stance, his weight perfectly balanced to react to an attack from any quarter.

"You have news?"

+++ I do, my lady. What we have long suspected has been proved at last. Parakka are here +++

Aurin did not even blink at the information. "Tell me what happened."

+++ We received word about a Resonant living among the Marginal community some time back. Complying with your orders to round up all the — +++

"My *father's* orders," she corrected tersely.

+++ My apologies. When we captured this Resonant, it was decided that he was a suitable candidate for . . . conversion +++ Tatterdemalion shifted uncomfortably. +++ After the process was complete, he revealed that he had been a Parakkan sympathizer, and that he had arranged to meet with them a short while before we took him. He suspected that his brother would continue his attempt +++

"And you saw a chance to locate the Parakkans and follow them back to their hideout," Aurin finished.

+++ I misjudged the new recruit +++ Tatterdemalion buzzed amid a crackle of static. +++ He retained a grudge of some kind against his brother. His intention was to ambush and kill him. We hid ourselves at the rendezvous, but he broke cover and gave us away. Our hand was forced. We attempted to kill or capture the Parakkans; but we suffered losses and were forced to withdraw +++

"And the new recruit?"

+++ He was executed for his actions +++ the Jachyra stated without emotion.

"Good."

Aurin turned away and went to the window, her fingers splayed across the sill as the cool wind stirred her hair. Tatterdemalion followed her uncertainly, loping across the room to stand a short way behind and to the left of her.

"Who knows of this?" she said at length.

+++ The Jachyra. No one else +++

"You will not tell my father." It was an order, not a question.

+++ Understood, my lady +++

She ran her fingertips across the cold gem lying against her collarbone. "How go things in the Dominions?"

+++ There was a little resistance to begin with, as you know. Since then, there has been nothing. Parakka is the most potent force against us, and they failed to hold us back. The combined forces of the Keriags and the Guardsmen have subjugated utterly the mainland Dominion civilization, excepting the sparsely populated steppes in the East and portions of the southern deserts. The nomadic folk of those places are difficult to find and bring to heel, but they are an insignificant threat and apparently too concerned with their own problems to oppose your father +++

"Oh yes," she said, with a hint of a smile. "The desert folk have the Sa'arin to worry about, and the Nomen have a hard enough time just surviving. Doubtless they still prefer their primitive existence to my father's rule."

+++ **Doubtless** +++ Tatterdemalion agreed neutrally.

"And besides, he hasn't *utterly* subjugated anything," Aurin said. "The Machinists' guild remain autonomous, and the Deliverers remain free."

+++ **The Machinists are a mercenary organization, and will work for whoever pays them. Your father sees no need to waste the manpower in bringing them under his heel** +++

Aurin laughed, low and humorless. "Or perhaps he thinks he can't penetrate the Citadel? I should imagine he will find that something of a task if he tries, yes?"

+++ **Possible. I am merely reporting his words** +++

"I'm sorry, Tatterdemalion. Please go on," she said, glancing over her shoulder at him.

+++ The Deliverers remain a mystery, both as to where they come from and how they operate. The King is intending to implement a system similar to the one in Kirin Taq, to choke off the supply of spirit-stones to those not of noble blood, or in the employ of those nobles. That will make the Deliverers next to redundant, except to service his future troops and allies. He will seize the mines, and make it treason for a commoner to have stones. It will crush once and for all the chance of rebellion. But it will take time +++

Aurin was silent for some while, her eyes focused on the middle distance, looking out over the half-lit realm that she ruled. Meaningless, all of it. She cared nothing for the realm, nothing for the tracts of land that the people clutched for, nothing for the pathetic little insects that scurried about in their useless jobs and pointless lives.

+++ And the uprising in Kitika, my Lady? +++

"Uprising?" she laughed. "Please don't grace it with so grand a title. A few traitorous bandits in an insignificant little manufacturing town hardly constitutes an uprising, yes?"

+++ I informed you of its beginnings two cycles ago. I think it unwise to leave a decision any longer +++

She sighed, as if bothered by the troublesome incon-

venience of a reply. "Send some of my father's Guardsmen. Take the Jachyra to be sure nobody escapes. Kill
the rebels. Send their families to the mines. Then kill the
ruling council for allowing the cancer of dissent to
thrive in their town." She paused, then added as an af-
terthought. "Kill their families, too."

**+++ And what will you have me do about Parakka,
my lady? +++**

"I will deal with Parakka," she said, the faintest wisp
of a smile crossing her face.

5

Windows into the Past

The Rifts ran along the edge of the Fin Jaarek mountain range, hugging the eastern shores of Kirin Taq's waist. The name was given to a vast stretch of dense forest that hid a network of valleys, canyons, and shattered terrain beneath its cool, dark foliage. Sections of land would suddenly plunge hundreds of feet to a plain many miles across, and deep, bottomless cracks zigzagged unpredictably across the ground. It was a hostile place, populated by all kinds of beasts that had thrived in the environment and adapted to be as hostile as their surroundings. The Kirins steered clear of it, preferring the mountains to the east or the plains to the west. Only a few isolated collectives of people lived there, those who were willing to brave the vicious world that the Rifts offered in exchange for rich land and relative freedom from Aurin's rule.

One such isolated collective was Parakka.

Hochi sat on the edge of his sleeping pallet, his huge shoulders and back outlined in the orange light of the glowstone in the bracket behind him. His face was in shadow, his heavy brow creased sternly as he contemplated the tiny object in his massive hand. It was a small silver pendant, its thin chain curled haphazardly across his palm. It was wrought in the shape of the hollow corona of the Kirin Taq sun, with a symbol set in the circular gap in its center. Hochi had been gazing at it for a long time, studying the swirls and curves that made up its shape. Tochaa's parting gift to him, entrusted to his care as the Kirin died in his arms in the Ley Warren during Parakka's doomed battle to prevent the Integration.

A year now, and he still had no idea what it meant.

The pendant represented many things to him. Guilt, first and foremost. Tochaa had lost his own life defending Hochi from the Keriags, when Hochi had never treated him as he deserved; he had seen only the grey skin of a Kirin, instead of the man beneath, and it had taken Tochaa's death to make him see otherwise. It also represented the promise he had sworn, to introduce Parakka to the Kirin people, to help them raise themselves from under the yoke of Macaan's family. That was the job he had dedicated himself to for the past year, and he had worked tirelessly at it. But it wasn't enough. He still felt that he was missing the true nature of the task that Tochaa had given to him; and the answer was there, in his hand, if he could only see it. . . .

"Hey, Uncle Hochi!" Elani chimed as she swung around the doorframe and propelled herself into the room. She entered the room at a run, but his heavy mood and lack of response caused her to slow down, her smile fading, until she came to a halt next to him.

"I'm sorry, did I bring you down, Elani?" he asked, giving her a halfhearted smile.

"'Course not, Uncle Hochi," came the depressed reply. "Whatcha doin'?"

Hochi slipped the pendant back over his bull neck; it was a little too tight for him, but he was fortunate that Tochaa had worn it loose. "Thinking, I suppose."

"Careful," she warned.

"Thanks."

She sat down on the pallet next to him and huffed out a sigh. "You've been doing too much thinking recently, Uncle Hochi. I never get to see you."

"I'm busy, Elani. You know how much work it takes to

keep an organization like this running? Just coordinating the different groups is —"

"*I'd* be busy if you'd let me go with the others when they're out recruiting," she said pedantically.

"You know you can't," he replied. "Besides, you're one of our only Resonants. You're too valuable to risk, even if I let you." Elani looked at him hopefully. "Which I *wouldn't*," he added, watching her face fall.

"Why do I have to be valuable?" she moaned. "Can't I be expendable, like Gerdi?"

"Gerdi's not expendable, he's just a pain in the —"

"Hold it, boss-man, or you'll say something you regret," came a voice from the doorway, and the subject of their conversation sauntered in, wearing a wry grin under his shock of green hair.

"Oh good," murmured Hochi sarcastically. "Just what I need."

"Hi, Gerdi!" Elani beamed. Hochi and Gerdi's weird relationship never ceased to amuse her. They both expended so much effort on disguising the affection they felt for each other, when it was plainly transparent to everyone that there was a deep respect between them.

He saluted her smartly. "How you goin', Elani?"

"I'm bored," she moaned, pulling a maudlin face.

71

"Then I've got just the thing for you," Gerdi declared. He cast a look over at Hochi and added: "You, too, Hoch. You've been sitting on that pallet for so long it's starting to warp under you. Not that it'd *take* long."

Hochi didn't even bother rising to it. He wasn't in the mood for one of Gerdi's endless routines of jabs about his weight or his huge belly.

"Whew," Gerdi said, throwing up his hands. "If *I* got that much enthusiasm on *my* return from the north, I'd go and join Aurin instead of hanging around with you lot."

"They're *back*?" Elani cried, jumping excitedly to her feet.

"Uh-huh. Sighted on the clifftops. They'll be here any minute."

"Come on, Uncle Hochi!" she said, grabbing his hand, her small fingers dwarfed in his wide palm. He heaved himself off the edge of the pallet, wincing slightly as the wound in his leg twinged. It was a souvenir from the Integration, when a Keriag had plunged a *gaer bolga* spear through his thigh; because of the hooked serrations on the spear, it had never really healed properly. Sighing, he allowed himself to be led outside.

Base Usido was Parakka's core of operations in Kirin

Taq. Given the short amount of time that they'd had to set it up, it had flourished fast over the year since its inception; but its success had been dearly bought. The Rifts were a dangerous place, and many lives had been lost during the construction of the defenses that ringed its edges. Even now, they could not afford to relax their guard against the dangers of the Rifts; but it was a necessary sacrifice, for only in a place like this could Parakka have remained undetected for so long.

It was as if the ground had been stamped in by some immense, misshapen foot. An enormous section of the forest floor, spanning many leagues, seemed to have simply dropped three hundred feet down from the surrounding land and formed an inverted plateau, a great plain surrounded by miles of sheer cliffs. The perimeter of Base Usido ran out in a semicircle from one such stretch of cliffs, swallowing up hundreds of acres of the grassy blue plain that it sat on. Its walls borrowed something of their design from those used in the stockades of Os Dakar; the high stone barricade was surrounded by a lethal brace of metal stakes, angled upwards and outward.

Hochi's hut was only one of many cut from the flexible, dark red wood of the abundant haaka trees. It sat in a cluster near one of the cliffs that rose at the back of Base

73

Usido, a wall that thrust upwards so high that it seemed to lean over the group of buildings beneath it. Its stone skin was impregnated with lifts, winches, and pulleys, allowing access to the clifftop fortifications that defended the rear of the settlement.

As they stepped outside, they entered the never-ceasing atmosphere of industry that the Base operated under. Nearby, a courtyard and a group of small offices formed the wyvern-pens; three of the magnificent creatures waited there now, their double-pairs of wings folded at their side, shifting their weight expectantly on their immensely muscular legs. The riders on their backs, lying against the wyverns' bony spines in padded harnesses, were being instructed by somebody on the ground; but a high wooden wall obscured him or her from view. As they watched, one of the wyverns bunched its squat body and then lunged upwards, leaping a clear fifty feet, its split tail trailing behind it. Then it spread its wings, the huge ones at the back opening out before the smaller forewings, and propelled itself upwards with a screech towards the sky.

"When is Cousin Ryushi getting Bonded?" Elani asked, reminded by the sight. "He's always going on about becoming a rider, getting to have his own wyvern companion that only he can fly."

"Not till he comes of age," Hochi said. "Those are the rules. He only has another year to wait."

"A *year*? But —"

"Getting Bonded is not as straightforward as it looks, Elani," Hochi said, his deep voice smoothing over her high squeak. "To have a mental link that close with another creature, it's a big responsibility. Wyverns are intelligent creatures too. They have their own will. It's not just a matter of control, it's a kind of kinship. Even Bonding at your eighteenth winter is too early sometimes. Kia and Ryushi's father gave them Bonding-stones a long time ago, and I argued with him then about it. In his place, I have to look out for them. I owe him that much." He paused. "They haven't come of age yet, Elani, and until then I won't let them complicate their lives further with something like Bonding."

"*O-kay*, I just asked," Elani sighed, wearied by the long explanation.

As they went further through the Base, they passed more evidence of the self-sufficiency of the colony; a steam-driven sawmill; a small, crude hatchery; a training field; a water pump and a small reservoir; a longhouse similar to the one in Gar Jenna, their old hideout in the Dominions. Most of the metal had been cannibalized from the war-machines that had survived the battle at the Ley Warren, and assembled by those Machinists that worked for Parakka. It was not an easy life in Base Usido, but it was better than for many who lived outside the Rifts.

They reached the main gate just as it was being winched closed behind the new arrivals, screeching as its two metal halves slid together on vast rollers. Six riders were dismounting from their pakpaks, passing their tethers to handlers who waited to stable the tired beasts. They had come down to the plain via one of the many mechanical haulage lifts that dotted the edges of the cliffs, and ridden the rest of the way to the gate. Now, as Elani saw them, she let out a whoop of excitement and ran up to her "cousin," Ryushi. He was one of her wide range of adopted family members, which included Kia, Hochi, and the twins' dead father Banto.

"Hey, El," he said wearily, as she launched herself into his arms and hugged him. She squeezed him tight for a few moments, before it dawned on her that Ryushi's reciprocation was only half-hearted.

"What's wrong?" she queried, drawing back so her wide eyes could search his.

"We've got trouble," he said gravely. "Aurin knows we're here. We gotta call the Council."

* * *

The longhouse was silent as Kia sat down again, her red hair aglow in the flickering light. Her report of the incident at Mon Tetsaa had given everyone something to digest, both the Council members that sat in a circle around the deep firepit and those that stood beyond the glow, where the torches had been purposely extinguished to emphasize their noninvolvement. Everyone was allowed to listen to the Council; but those that had not been elected were only allowed to speak at the Council's discretion. Until then, they had to stand outside the island of light in the dim blackness.

Kia shifted herself slightly on the wicker mat that she sat on, her green eyes moving from one Council member to another, awaiting their response. Age was of no importance in Parakka — a person was judged on their merits, not on their experience — and at least a quarter of the members were under twenty winters in Dominion-time. A good proportion of the Council were Kirins, too, when there had been none before the Integration. Times had changed. Since the Dominion-folk in Parakka had been flipped to Kirin Taq after the battle at the Ley Warren, the majority of their subsequent numbers had been made up of the native people. Her eyes fell finally on Calica, meeting her gaze levelly across the sullen coals of the firepit.

"It seems, then," said the Convener, a gaunt Dominion man with lank white hair, "that our time has suddenly grown short."

"I disagree," came another voice. Unsurprisingly, it was a young Kirin called Baki who protested. He always played the opposing viewpoint, even when he did not believe it himself. It was his way of balancing both sides of an argument. "So Aurin knows we're here in Kirin Taq. I have no doubt that she suspected all along; our spies have reported much the same from what they have gathered in the cities. But she doesn't know where we're hiding. She still can't find us. We're in no greater danger here than we were before, and we shouldn't rush things. We have to be more careful, and that means *not* hurrying."

"Two seasons ago, that would have been true," Calica said, still maintaining her habit of marking time Dominion-style. "But not now. The few free Resonants that we have managed to make contact with tell us that Macaan has the Dominions well under his power now. That's largely thanks to his taking a large portion of Aurin's army of Keriags with him. Soon he won't need them anymore, and Aurin can recall her troops and use them to scour every inch of Kirin Taq until they find this place."

"We should bolster our defenses around the Rifts, then," said one of the other members.

"Well, that goes without saying —" someone else began, but Kia suddenly interrupted him.

"What's the *point*?" she cried, silencing everyone for the second time. "You can't defend against the Keriags. Not with what we've got. We don't even have our war machines anymore. We scrapped them all to get the raw materials to build this place. Wasting time and resources on trying to stop those things is just senseless. If the Keriags get to Base Usido and we're still here, we all die. It's that simple."

Her pronouncement took a few moments to sink in. She glared at Baki, daring him to contradict her. The other members of the Council were recalling what they knew of the creatures called the Keriags. Most of the Kirins had seen them firsthand; to the Dominion-folk, they were largely known only by their fearsome reputation. Tireless, insectile warriors, endless in number and near-unstoppable, they had been responsible for the deaths of many of Parakka's troops during the Integration.

"I assume you have a —" the Convener began. He was about to say *suggestion,* but Kia talked over him.

"Yeah, I *do*," she replied hotly. She had everybody's

ear now. "We've been trying ever since the Integration to investigate Aurin's hold over the Keriags, to work out why they obey her. It's not worked. The Jachyra are too smart, and they keep our spies out of her palace. It's a miracle none have been caught trying to get in and interrogated. So we need a new angle. I want to go and try the Koth Taraan."

A murmur rippled around the darkness outside the firelight. Kia had explained what they had learned about the creatures during her report, and relayed what Taacqan had told her about them.

"But the Koth Taraan are mindless beasts. You said so yourself," the Convener stated.

"Yeah, that's what Taacqan told me. He was very clear on the point. In fact, he made a little *too* much effort to make out that they were mindless and violent. But when Peliqua and Jaan had a run-in with them, they didn't seem like either. I think he was keeping something from us, for one reason or another." She rubbed the back of her neck. "I think he might have been protecting them. I don't think I'd have realized any of this, but for what he said to Ty at the end. He said something about the Koth Taraan and the Keriags. I don't know what that meant exactly —"

"It's something of a tenuous reason for travelling all

the way back to the Unclaimed Lands, don't you think?" Baki interrupted derisively.

"As an alternative to sitting on my hands in Base Usido and getting massacred, I think it's pretty good," she replied, smiling sweetly at him.

"Now hey, nobody's sitting on their hands!" protested another member.

"That's all we *have* been doing!" Kia cried. "We've been maintaining the illusion of doing a lot and getting nowhere. And there's no time for that anymore. I'm gonna try something different. Alone if I have to, but I think it would greatly increase my chances if some others were to come along with me. *If*, of course, the honorable Council will allow it." She said this last sentence in a tone that suggested she was going whether they liked it or not. The motion was voted on and carried.

Other things were discussed that night, including what they had learned of the Jachyra from the events that had occurred at Mon Tetsaa. Taacqan's brother was a Resonant, that they knew. And if he was to be believed, the Jachyra that had killed him had been his brother also. What, then, had happened in the meantime? Were *all* the Jachyra Resonants? Did that explain their ability to pass through mirrors; was it some kind of twist on their natural abilities? Conjecture and guesswork, and no solid proof. There was little that could be done. Baki made a new call to send their best spies to Fane Aracq to try and infiltrate Aurin's palace, but the motion was denied. Too many chances had been taken that way already. They needed somebody on the inside, needed it *desperately;* but there seemed to be no way of *getting* there.

Days passed in the Dominions, but in Kirin Taq it was only the repetitive cycle of colors within the abundant patches of Glimmer plants that told of the passing of time. Preparations were being made for Kia's trip north, along with the multitude of other missions that had been forced into action by the incident at Mon Tetsaa. Messengers were leaving for all corners of the land; diplomats were being sent to the tribes in the Rifts to ne-gotiate their support; the wyverns' breeding program was being stepped up, and new blood needed to be im-ported, so merchants had gone to buy battle-wyverns. The defenses were being shored up, also, for despite Kia's protest against that motion she had been voted down. Like the Convener had said, time had suddenly grown short, and everyone in Base Usido was keenly aware of the fact.

"Hey, sis," Ryushi said, materializing at Kia's shoulder as she adjusted the saddle on a pakpak. She jumped and swore, and the pakpak crabbed away nervously. Ryushi caught its reins, and Kia soothed it for a moment before turning to her brother.

"You scared me," she said with an embarrassed smile.

"Didn't mean to," he replied. She could tell by his expression that there was something he wanted to talk to her about. They were twins, even if they hadn't acted like it for a long while, and she knew him better than anyone.

She glanced up at her pakpak. "You wanna go for a ride?"

"In the Rifts? Not too safe," Ryushi said.

"You think *we* need to be worried?" she asked, goading him.

"Not really," he admitted. "I just thought I'd say."

"Go get a ride and saddle up, then. I'll race you out."

Ryushi returned shortly with a mount of his own, and they cantered their pakpaks to the gate in silence. Once the lookouts had pronounced the plain beyond all clear, they were allowed to leave. The gate began to slide noisily shut behind them.

"When the gate closes, we go," Kia said. "First to the mottled cliff."

"I'll have a fire ready when you get there," Ryushi grinned.

The gate clanged shut, and they dug their heels into the leathery flanks of their mounts. The pakpaks' strong hind legs gave them extraordinary acceleration, and they sprinted across the plain at a staggering pace. The wind blew the twins' hair into whirls, pushing at their faces and shoulders as the blue-black grass beneath them was eaten up by the long strides of the pakpaks. Kia, bent low against the neck of her mount, yelled in exhilaration as she began to outpace her brother. The beasts skipped along the plain, their two-toed feet propelling them forward in low bounds, their tiny front limbs hugged close to their chests.

The race lasted only a few minutes, but to the twins it seemed longer in the rush of adrenaline. Ryushi had come to enjoy these windows into the past that he shared with his sister, when everything between them was as it had been before their father had been killed. There were precious few of them nowadays. When they eventually came to a stop, Kia had beaten him soundly, and had already dismounted by the time he pulled up next to her.

"No fair; you chose the faster one," he said breathlessly.

"Half of winning is forward planning, bro," she replied.

The mottled cliff was a section of the towering walls around Base Usido that was covered in patches of a curious green-brown fungus that held a dim luminescence in the twilight of Kirin Taq. They settled at its foot, after checking as far as they could along the plain for anything dangerous about. The only signs of life were a flock of bright wading-birds, shadowy outlines in a nearby pool.

"So, you decided if you're coming with me yet?" Kia prompted as they lay half-reclined on the grass, chests heaving with the exertion of the ride. The pakpaks, nearby, had taken to cropping grass in the way they always did when left unattended for more than thirty seconds. "You've only got a cycle left to decide."

"Yeah," he said. "I'm not."

"Oh," said Kia, sounding a little surprised and disappointed. "Okay."

There was silence.

"Is this about Calica?" she asked.

"Why should it be?" he replied.

"Well, you do spend an awful lot of time with her. . . ."

"I don't seem to have anyone else to spend it with, now do I?" Ryushi was unable to keep the accusation out of his voice.

"You're sore about something," Kia said, lying back on the grass.

"Yeah, now that you mention it, I am," he replied. "Am I still your brother or what?"

"'Course you are," she said, frowning. "What kind of —"

"No, you don't seem to get me. *Takami's* our brother, but he's also a murdering, honorless bag of filth. I mean more than a biological brother, more than a brother in name only."

Kia raised herself up on her elbows and sighed. "Stop dancing around the subject and tell me what you're getting at."

"We don't act like twins anymore, Kia. We'd barely pass the grade as friends. *Acquaintances* is more like it." Ryushi looked out over the plain, his eyes becoming distant. "We didn't *used* to be acquaintances."

"A lot's changed since then," Kia replied quietly. "People have died."

"*We* haven't," Ryushi shot back. "It's — oh, there's no point to this. It's not like this conversation is gonna alter anything, is it? You've got Ty now, anyway. What do you need with a brother?"

"Is *that* what this is about? And what've you been doing with Calica, you hypocrite?"

"I've gotta spend my time with *someone,*" Ryushi argued. "What do you expect? You've been icing me out for the last year."

"Yeah, but *Calica* . . ." she said, a hint of something distasteful in the word.

Ryushi got to his feet and turned on her angrily. "What is your *problem* with her? You think you can shut your own twin out of your life and then reserve the right to judge what he does? Uh-uh, it doesn't work like that. You forfeited all that a long time ago."

"What do you see in her?" Kia cried, rising with him. Their conversation had degenerated into a shouting match by now, such as they had not had in a long time. "I mean, what is she, really?"

"She's a *friend,*" he replied.

Kia laughed, genuine amusement in her eyes. "You really believe that? *Please.* Anyone can see how you are about each other."

"And how's that?" Ryushi asked scornfully.

"Figure it out," she replied.

There was a long moment as they glared at each other, challenging. Then Ryushi's lips twisted into a sarcastic curl.

"You're jealous, aren't you?" he said.

"Of her? As *if*," Kia shot back, but the denial was not strong enough to be convincing. Besides, there was something more than that, there had *always* been something more. A feeling she couldn't pin down about Calica that —

"After what you've done with Ty, cutting me out for him, you're jealous of me doing the same to you!" Ryushi accused, barging into her thoughts. "And you call *me* a hypocrite. You can't have it both ways, sis. That's pathetic. Other people have got their lives to lead, y'know."

With that, he took a few steps' run-up and vaulted onto the saddle of his pakpak, which grunted in vague surprise and raised its head from the grass.

"For the record, I think this Koth Taraan thing is a wild-goose chase," he said. "And even if I didn't, I wouldn't go with you. Back home you always made out you were the mature one, sis. I think it's your turn to grow up now."

He spurred the pakpak and was away before she could reply, racing across the plains back towards Base

Usido, under the hollow glare of the dark sun high above him. His sister dwindled behind him, but he never turned back to look as she watched him go. His head was full of anger, not only at her but also at himself. He was as bad as she was. After all that he had said about leaving him out of her life, he had held something back himself. There was another reason why he wasn't going with her.

A message had arrived for him at Base Usido. The spy had brought it to Calica, and she had told him. A stranger had been travelling the towns, asking for Ryushi by name. The stranger wanted to meet him. The stranger had important information, but he would not speak to anyone except Ryushi.

The stranger said a name.

The name was Takami.

6

A Dishonest Bone

"You do know, of course, that this is a trap," Calica said, brushing the orange-gold cascade of her hair behind her ear and studying her companion.

She and Ryushi rode slowly away from the mechanical lift that had brought them up the sheer side of the valley. They spared nods for the operators and guards as they stepped off the wide metal platform, pushing through the wheezing clouds of steam that rose up from the pressure-brakes. Their pakpaks snuffed and grunted as they picked their way into the dark undergrowth, brown eyes uneasy. Whether by smell or by instinct, they knew the dangers of the Rifts, and they would rather not leave the sanctuary of Base Usido to head through the trackless depths of the forest.

"Course it's a trap," he replied, once they had gone a little way in. "Frankly, I'm kinda disappointed in Aurin. I thought she'd try harder."

"And you're still going? Why?"

"Because the Princess knows I'm not gonna turn down a chance — *any* chance — to get to him."

"Takami? Look, I know how you feel about him, but setting yourself up like this isn't going to get you any closer to what you want."

"What I *want* is to see his head on a burning post," Ryushi replied, his voice entirely serious. "But that's beside the point. How could I pass up this opportunity, if there's even the slightest possibility I could get to him? I'm honor-bound to avenge my father. You know that."

"Sure, I know that. And so does Aurin. That's why she's using it against you."

Ryushi made a shrug of concession, as if to say: *so be it*, and the discussion was over.

Calica turned her attention back to the trail. She knew how eaten up Ryushi was about this whole affair. Ever since he had duelled with his older brother in the dark tunnels of the Ley Warren, he had been obsessed with exacting revenge for their father's death. After all, it was Takami's treachery that had plunged them from their safe existence in the mountains into the violent reality of war in the first place. Several times Ryushi had tried to find a way to reach his enemy, to force an end to their blood-feud; but Takami was a noble now, Takami-*kos* of the province of Maar. He was too well-guarded to get near. It frustrated Ryushi, and she saw that; but it was beginning to get out of hand, if he intended to go along with such a blatant trap as the one they faced.

Bizarrely, Kia's reaction to the news that Takami was the killer of their father had been far less extreme than Ryushi's. They had waited for her to recover from the near-fatal weakness she had inflicted upon herself during the battle at the Ley Warren before breaking it to her; but even so, she did not seem to be cut nearly so deeply by the revelation as her twin. Perhaps all her hate was already invested in Macaan's men. Maybe her new love for Ty had calmed her somewhat. But whatever the reasoning behind it, the idea of revenge on Takami had not become her first priority as it had with Ryushi; though Calica had no doubt that Kia would not hesitate to grasp any opportunity to get hold of her treacherous older brother.

"Look, I'm just going there to meet with this person," Ryushi said, mistaking her contemplation for sulky disapproval. "It'll be on neutral ground. There's not much chance of an ambush, and if there were . . ." he shrugged, "we can handle 'em. But all I know so far is that this guy is mouthing off about wanting to meet me, and that he has something on Takami. I can't just let it rest at that. Once I meet him, and we find out what the whole story is, *then* I'll decide if I'm gonna go with it."

Calica gave him a sidelong glance. "As if I believe *that*," she said. "Your mind's made up already."

They rode on, and the Glimmer shards that they carried in their belts pulsed from red to indigo to violet. Base Usido was close to the edge of the Rifts, but not so close that it didn't take a half-cycle or more to get onto open land. They were kept constantly wary, for even though their route was through the less dangerous areas of the Rifts, staying on the high plateaus, it was still far from safe. As their journey progressed, Calica dropped back a little, slowing imperceptibly until she was a few feet behind Ryushi and out of the range of his peripheral vision. Ryushi, keeping his eyes on the doleful trees around him, did not notice her doing it; and his attention was too focused to notice her olive gaze on him, studying the side of his face as she had done so many times before, her mind distracted by something other than the dangers of the Rift beasts.

She didn't know when it had happened. Even when she pressed herself, she could not pinpoint the moment when her friendship and respect for her companion had shifted violently to love. Perhaps there had always been a smoldering ember there somewhere, waiting to ignite the rest of her. She remembered when he came to her quarters in the canyon hideout of Gar Jenna, back in the Dominions. She remembered how he had impulsively hugged her upon their return from Os Dakar, and how the hug had seemed to hold . . . well, more than friendship. Those moments had happened over a year ago, and at the time she had thought little of them. But now . . .

It didn't matter. However, whenever it had happened, it *had* happened. And she had to deal with it.

Unfortunately, that was turning out to be the hard part.

The trouble was, she didn't know his mind. She was unable to read the signals. Eighteen winters had passed in her life, but like many in Parakka she had grown up hard and fast since she lost her parents to Macaan. She was a strong warrior, a respected tactician; she had become the head of the Tusami City chapter of Parakka before she had even come of age. Her life had been a fight to be the best, and it had left precious little time for such intangibles as romance. She had been perfectly happy to get by without that particular hindrance; but she had reckoned without the overwhelming insistence of the emotions that harried her now. She had assumed that she had a choice where love was concerned, but circumstances had proved her wrong.

Her psychometry was no use, either. It gave her only surface detail; and the one thing she never seemed to be able to find out was how Ryushi felt about *her*. Perhaps it was because it meant so much to her that she could not glean it from him, in the same way that an important show could make a performer so nervous that they were unable to do what they had done a hundred times in rehearsal.

It seemed the simplest thing, just to tell him how she felt and be done with all the torture that she put herself through. The simplest thing, but somehow her pride would not allow her to form the words in her mouth.

Calica's spirit-stones worked both ways, though neither was very reliable. As well as the past, she occasionally grasped flashes of the future as they flickered across her subconscious mind. It was such a flash that interrupted her thoughts and caused her to whisper an alert to Ryushi.

"What is it?" he asked, looking over his shoulder at her, one hand on the hilt of his sword. They were in an area where the trees had become sparser, pushing their way through rocky ground, and the faint light from the dark sun filtered through the leaf canopy a little stronger than usual, painting everything a dim pastel blue.

"Something's coming," she said urgently. "Get out of sight! Over there!"

They wheeled their pakpaks together and rode them as fast as they dared to where a screen of star-thorn bushes grew on the fringe of a shallow, stony dip in the land. They pulled their mounts to a halt behind the cover, the pakpak's feet crunching and scratching on loose gravel, and settled to wait, searching the forest for a sign of what Calica had sensed.

It was not long in coming. First there was a short fizzle of soft blue-white light, which glowed and died almost as soon as Ryushi noticed it. Then another, darting round the gnarled bole of a haaka tree and extinguishing itself, quick as an eyeblink. Then two together, wheeling in perfect formation and disappearing. Then more, and more, until finally there were hundreds of the things, fat tadpoles of light that were being slowly drawn together, appearing in the darkness and crawling towards a central core of light, which glowed brighter as more of the ghostly arrivals joined it. The air was filled with a sharp whispering noise, the sound of a thousand hushed voices in unison, but Ryushi was unable to make out any words amid the subdued clamor.

"Bane?" he asked, his eyes fixed on the congealing mass.

"Bane," Calica agreed.

And then the mass began to take shape and form, elongating and solidifying until it was almost eel-like, with a frill of ethereal energy running down its narrow sides, and a face that had no eyes but only a wide, blind mouth. Trailing sparkling blobs of blue-white light in its wake, it wound its way off through the trees, curving and arcing and rolling and diving between the boughs, until its illumination had faded from sight.

"That's the third one I've seen recently," Calica murmured gravely. "I don't like it."

"Why?" Ryushi asked. "They never go near the other settlements in the Rifts. They're no trouble."

"The other settlements are full of Kirins," Calica said, edging her pakpak out of hiding. It responded with a snort. "Base Usido has a lot of Dominion-folk. That's a lot of spirit-stones."

"So what?"

Calica scratched the back of her forearm anxiously. "There've been developments since you left for Mon Tetsaa. All the reports show that there are more Banes than ever before now, and they all seem to be heading for Base Usido. Banes only form when there's something to feed on. We figure it's the energy from the spirit-stones they're looking for."

"Yeah, but they're scavengers; they're too weak to — "

"It's not *them* I'm worried about," Calica interrupted. "It's the packs of Snagglebacks that follow them around. And with the Snagglebacks, you get the Snappers. I'm sure you remember *them*."

Ryushi made a tiny nod. He remembered them well enough; Os Dakar had been crawling with them.

"Something's brewing," she said distantly. "I'm just worried about it. Perhaps we should go back and warn the Base."

"*You* can," Ryushi said. "I've got an appointment to keep."

For a moment, Calica hesitated, caught in a choice between satisfying her niggling worries or staying with the one she reluctantly loved. But it was only a moment, for in the end there was no contest. With an inward sigh of resignation, she turned her pakpak and made ready to travel on.

The Votive Grove stood on the western edge of the Rifts, a mile or so beyond where the ground finally gave up its chaotic jumbling and smoothed itself into grassland. It stood alone, a cluster of exactly one hundred tall, straight trees that towered high and curved in on themselves to form a vast natural dome of blue leaves shot through with sparkling seams of crystal. The trunks of the trees formed the pillars to this colossal place, which had been standing for longer than any could remember. Legend had it that it had been created by a great King of long ago, as a monument to the son who tried to have him assassinated. Before he was put to death, the son was granted a final request, as was customary for royalty; he asked that the King leave something marking his memory that would stand for eternity, and so the Votive Grove was planted.

That was but one legend. Many others had sprung up since then, so much so that the place was rarely visited now. It was a haunted place, where evil spirits and Banes dwelt. But evil spirits had no need for fires, and Ryushi could see the spasmodic flicker of a blaze between the pillars of bark, throwing the short, dancing shadows of the trunks onto the grass outside the grove.

"Someone's home," Calica observed needlessly.

Ryushi didn't reply. He patted the neck of his pakpak absently and then nudged it into a trot, heading towards the grove. Calica followed, her hand resting on the hilt of her katana.

All was still as they passed between the immense pillars and into the shelter of the arched canopy of knitted branches. A shallow stone firepit was in the exact center of the Votive Grove, and a bonfire had been built up in it. The deep, gruff purring of the burning wood was the only sound aside from the animal noises of their pakpaks and the periodic clink of their scabbards tapping against their saddle buckles.

They waited for a moment, but there was no sign of whoever had built the fire.

"Is anyone there?" Calica called, her voice swallowed by the leafy dome.

"'Course," came the reply from the darkness outside. "Think that fire built itself?"

They reined around and saw a shadow leaning against one of the trunks, a smaller shadow by its side. Standing just on the edge of the firelight, it was impossible to make out exactly who it was.

"Well, we're here," said Ryushi, squinting at the stranger.

"I was thinking you weren't gonna show," came the reply. "Then I thought, well, if you saw me here it might put you off and you'd turn and get before you heard me out."

I know that voice, Ryushi thought. *It's been a year, but . . .*

"Whist?" he queried tentatively.

"Pretty sharp, Ryushi," he said, stepping into the fire-light. Blink loped along next to him, his huge, rangy grey dog. He hadn't changed much since last time Ryushi had seen him. He still went barechested, with his lean body covered in swirling skin-dye designs that crawled up his neck and around his cheeks and face and eyes. His hair was still bunched and spiked and hanging, a mishmash of styles and colors, and he still wore the thick metal glove on one hand that he used for throwing the razor discs on his belt. No, he hadn't changed much. It was just that he was *supposed* to be dead. And Ryushi wasn't certain that he wouldn't have preferred it that way.

"I thought Ty took care of you back in Os Dakar," he said, sliding his sword free from its scabbard. Calica followed suit, controlling with her knees her nervy pak-pak's attempts to sidestep.

"Well, y'know, reports of my death have been greatly exaggerated, and all that stuff," Whist replied offhand-edly, walking across the grass towards where they stood by the fire. "You really wanna know the details?"

"Indulge me," Ryushi replied. "And stay where you are."

"Seems I heard that line first time we met," Whist said, halting obediently and squatting down to scratch under Blink's chin. "Kirin guy, Tochaa, said that. How's he doing, anyway?"

"He's dead," Ryushi replied.

"Really? Shame," Whist said thoughtfully. "He was uptight, but I kinda liked him." He shook his head, aware that he had drifted. "Oh yeah, sorry. You wanted to know why I'm here, and not dead after falling off that stupid big machine, huh? Well, Blink here wasn't too keen on meeting the ground at that kinda speed, so he winked out to a safer spot. And seeing as we were sorta entangled, he took me with him." He nuzzled the massive dog, which licked his nose. "I'd seen Flicker Dogs like him disappear with food in their mouths before, back in the Wildlands. Guess I didn't think he could transport a whole human. Proved me wrong." He grinned at them.

Ryushi glanced at Blink, remembering Kia's story of how they had gotten into the Fallen Sun stockade on Os Dakar. Flicker Dogs could wink themselves over distances without crossing the intervening ground, simply popping out of nowhere.

"Anyway," Whist concluded. "I hid out while the Keriags trashed the settlement. There's not much left of it now. After that, when they thought there was no one still alive, it was easy enough to get off the plateau through the Guardsmen's corridors now I knew that Blink could get me there. I'm an enterprising kid." He stood up and stretched. "So there you are. And now I'm here. Satisfied?"

"What are you up to?" Ryushi asked, naked suspicion in his tone.

"Why did I get you to come here, you mean? Ah, that's pretty much the real question, isn't it? I wanna give you a present. See, I've been around a lot this past year, and I get to hear things, and I know you and your brother aren't exactly on great terms. Since he's become a thane, stories about him are all over. He —"

"Nobody outside of Parakka knew I was alive until ten cycles ago," Ryushi interrupted. "And only Aurin knew then. You're working for her, Whist. Don't insult me by pretending you're not."

Whist gave him an apologetic smile. "Sorry, but you haven't been keeping up on current affairs. Aurin circulated your description to every thane in Kirin Taq at least nine cycles ago. The Jachyra passed it on for her."

"So how did you find out?" Calica interceded.

"'Cause I work for *Takami*," he replied, getting faintly exasperated. "Not Aurin."

Ryushi's face became a sarcastic sneer in the shifting firelight. "That's even better, Whist. The one person on

Kirin Taq who is liable to want me dead more than Princess Aurin and you're working for him. You do know that if you try to ambush us now, I'll obliterate you and this whole grove?"

"This isn't an ambush," Whist replied. "Calm down, why don'tcha? I'm here to make you a deal. I can get you a shot at Takami." He paused for a moment, allowing his offer to sink in. "And in return, you let me into Parakka."

Ryushi's pakpak took a shifty step backwards; he automatically steadied it with the reins that were gathered in his left fist. "Come on, Whist. You betrayed my sister twice on Os Dakar. You think I'd even go along with your offer, let alone allow you to join Parakka?"

Blink growled at him, the sound low and throaty. Whist calmed his companion, running his gloved hand along the thick muscle of the massive dog's back. The two were linked by the power of Whist's spirit-stones, dog and boy in symbiosis. Ryushi had often wondered exactly how close their bond was, and its nature; but he was pretty sure that Blink's reaction reflected the emotion that Whist kept hidden.

"You're a smart kid, Ryushi," Whist said. "Obviously, I wasn't gonna expect you to agree just like that." He began to pace around at the edge of the circle of heat thrown out by the fire. "See, the thing is that you took it personal, what I did on Os Dakar. It wasn't personal. Me and Kettin had a deal; he left me alone, and I delivered any new arrivals to the plateau into his hands. It was his way of recruiting, y'know? Getting the cream of the bunch. Course, he had to find out if new kids were worth taking or not, and that was what the Snapper Run was all about. But it was just . . . that was my *deal*, see? Our arrangement." He looked up, his eyes meeting Ryushi's. "You saw what it was like on Os Dakar. We all did what we could to survive. Ask your friend Ty, ask him if *he* didn't have to compromise his morals to get by in that place."

"So what about Takami?" Ryushi asked, ignoring the reference to Ty because he knew it was true. "Why'd you choose him?"

"I didn't *choose* him," Whist replied, looking wounded. "He captured me. I had kind of a rough time after Os Dakar — the land around that place doesn't exactly get called hospitable, y'know? — and his guys picked me up and brought me to him."

"So, what, you got a deal going with him, too?" Calica asked.

"Like I said, I'm an enterprising kid," he shrugged. "Better that than rotting in a jail 'cause of my Dominion skin."

"And now you're betraying him, too," Ryushi said.

"Hey, it's not like I *asked* to be in his service. It was kind of a life-or-death decision." He looked at Blink, who growled sullenly. "I don't like being put in that position," he said. "He don't deserve no loyalty from me." Then he brightened. "But *you*," he said, pointing with his gloved hand. "I know you. You don't got a dishonest bone in your body. Otherwise you wouldn't have been so easy to sucker on Os Dakar. And when I heard about you, that you were still kickin', well, I thought: If there's one person who's gonna give my boss the payback he deserves, it's Ryushi, right?"

Nobody replied for a moment. Calica was watching Ryushi for a reaction.

"Anyway," Whist went on. "A guy like me has to cover himself. And if we make a deal, and Takami bites it . . . well, you're happy, but what about me? I'm out of a job, right? I need a safety net. And I'll tell you, I've had it with Aurin and her thanes. That leaves me with Parakka. All I ask is, if I get you to Takami, you forget about what I've done before and let me in."

His speech finished, Whist squatted back down next

to Blink, who was sitting to attention, watching Ryushi and Calica with interest.

Ryushi was silent.

"Tell me you're not seriously thinking of trusting this lying slime," Calica said.

Still Ryushi didn't reply, his face set in intense thought.

"I'll tell you what," Whist said, standing up. "I can see you need to work this out and make a decision. I'll be back here in two cycles. If you're not here, I'll assume the deal's off. If you are . . ." He grinned and left the sentence hanging.

"Ryushi . . ." Calica said, unable to quite believe he was giving serious credit to Whist's words.

"I'll see you both," Whist said, and with that he and his ever-present companion walked away, leaving the shelter of the Votive Grove into the twilight outside, rapidly fading from shadows into nothingness.

"Ryushi?" Calica prompted again.

Slowly, he tugged his pakpak around and began to head silently back towards the Rifts, and she could do nothing but follow.

7
Through the Gloom Until

The dank carpet of the Unclaimed Lands crept across the marshy earth beneath them. The Parakkans stood on a jutting ridge several miles to the northwest of Mon Tet-saa, their pakpaks cropping grass nearby with their flat teeth and rubbery lips. The thin clouds in the blue-purple sky held a faintly poisonous, greenish tinge, drifting across the face of the black abyss that was the sun. From somewhere beneath the wetland canopy, marsh-creatures gibbered and pipped. Rising above, knees and elbows of reddish rock slid out of the obscuring trees to dominate the landscape. A cool wind blew, swirling around them.

The Unclaimed Lands. The domain of the Koth Taraan.

"Well, it's not as if it's worse than the Rifts, is it?"

Peliqua said doubtfully. Her previous experience of the place meant that she wasn't keen on going back, but that still didn't quell her habit of finding a silver lining in every situation.

"That's only because we know what lives in the Rifts," Ty said. "We don't have any idea about this place."

"We know *one* thing that lives here," Kia stated.

"You're still sure you wanna do this, Kia?" Gerdi asked, one eye closed as he checked the sights on his crossbow.

"Never mess with a girl's intuition," she replied.

"Wouldn't dream of it," he said, slinging his crossbow back into its harness on his back. "How about you, Jaan?"

"Oh, I'm just raring to go," the halfbreed replied dismally.

"Yeah, I can tell," said Gerdi.

"None of us has trekked for two days — *cycles* — just to turn back now," Hochi said, his warhammer resting on his shoulder. "Let's get down there."

"Just remember," Kia said to them all. "We're supposed to be making contact. Don't get scared and attack anything. We don't fight unless they start it. Understand?"

"Unless your intuition is all off and they pulp us 'cause they really are as mindless as Taacqan said," Gerdi replied flippantly.

"Well, yeah, there is that," Kia mused. "Oh well, I suppose we gotta take the rough with the smooth. Come on."

They made their way down off the ridge and towards the Unclaimed Lands. After tethering their pakpaks in a sheltered nook and strapping feed-bags around the creatures' leathery underbellies, they unloaded their supplies and got ready to set off on foot. The wetland ground was too unstable for riding, even for surefooted pakpaks, and their mounts would undoubtedly end up stuck or lame if they took them in. They hesitated a moment at the border, each of them considering what they were getting themselves into; but the hesitation did not last long, and they forged on into the murky world of the Koth Taraan.

The atmosphere seemed to thicken instantly as they stepped into the wetlands. It was as if each of the knotted trees and bloated, dangling leaves sensed that they were intruders and frowned at them, weighing them down with disapproval. The high-pitched *kikiriki* of the marsh-rats was like the whine of blood in their ears, the frequency resting just on the top end of human hearing.

Distantly, a repetitive booming noise heralded the presence of something they would rather not meet. Many-legged leafcreepers wound their slow and sinister way through the branches, occasionally stringing themselves across the travellers' path as they crossed from tree to tree, so that they had to duck underneath the long, furred body and its small, hook-toed legs that scrabbled uselessly at the air. All around them, the wetlands crawled with life, and the terrain veered between unpleasant, treacherous, and downright lethal.

Gerdi nattered at Jaan as they walked, only half his mind on the trail. Jaan was characteristically uncommunicative, even around Gerdi, who, at thirteen winters, was only a little younger than the halfbreed. Gerdi usually tried to be friendly by bullying him out of his frequent dark moods, but Jaan would not ever really let the Noman boy near him; and while they could be called friends, they could not be called close.

"Keep alert, you two," said Hochi grouchily, after Gerdi had made a derisive comment to Jaan about the big man in a stage whisper that was loud enough to be overheard by everyone.

Peliqua couldn't be certain, but she thought that they had travelled further into the Unclaimed Lands than she and her brother had gotten before they made their first sighting. It was she who saw it first; she squealed excitedly and pointed before remembering that the Koth Taraan were supposed to be dangerous. It was a low shape against the background of one of the massive rocks that they had seen from the ridge, silent and unmoving. Had she not been looking out for it, she would have missed it completely. But though she tried to show the others, the only other person who could make it out in the dim light was Jaan, sharing as he did her Kirin vision.

"Are there any others?" Kia asked urgently.

"I can't see any," Peliqua said, scanning the surroundings with her cream-on-white eyes.

"Are you *sure* there's nothing there?" said Hochi, narrowing his eyes as he peered into the darkness.

"I *think* I — oh!"

"What?" Ty said quickly. "What is it?"

"It just moved," Jaan supplied in Peliqua's place.

"Guess that settles *your* hash," Gerdi said to Hochi. As the others continued talking, Hochi sidled nonchalantly over to him, with a view to clubbing him around the head; but Gerdi carefully positioned Peliqua between them so he could not get a clear shot.

"Where's it going?" Kia asked. "Is it coming towards us?"

Jaan squinted. "I think it's . . ." he began.

"It's moving away," Peliqua said. "Maybe it's going to tell the others we're here."

"Or go for reinforcements," Ty said.

Kia leaned on her bo staff. "Either way, they know we're around. We might as well keep on going. They'll come to us."

"Why do I not like that idea?" Gerdi murmured to himself.

The talking stopped after that. Everyone was far too intent on looking out for the Koth Taraan. Now that they knew they had been spotted, a confrontation was inevitable; but the real question was, would it be peaceful, or would it be a battle? Were the Koth Taraan beasts or beings? Questions and doubts preyed on their minds, for none of them were certain of anything about the creatures beyond their terrifying reputation, and none of them had any idea how they would handle the Koth Taraan if it came to a fight.

Time dragged, sucking at their feet like the swampy ground they travelled over. And still nothing happened. There was no sign of the Koth Taraan, and the Glimmer shards that they carried indicated that at least a half-cycle had passed since they had crossed the borders.

The going became steadily worse, so that each new step was uncertain; stable ground could suddenly turn into a wet sinkhole, or plunge them knee-deep in cold bog water. Vines grew thicker here, plucking at them with the tiny hooks on their leaves, attaching themselves like leeches; and the ground seemed to breathe a faint, chill mist that wound sinuously around their ankles. They were footsore and tired, covered in cold mud and soaked to the skin.

"Stop," said Kia, holding out a weary arm. They gratefully stumbled to a halt. "This is pointless. They're just letting us run ourselves ragged before they deal with us. We wait here. Make a camp."

"I don't think we're gonna need to," said Gerdi. "Look."

They were surrounded. Where the vast creatures had come from, Kia could not say; but this was their home ground, and they knew how to use it. This time, though they still kept just far enough away so that it was difficult to make out their form, they did not attempt to disguise their presence. They stood, some swaying, some hunched, some lumbering across the undergrowth; but they were there. The Koth Taraan.

"Okay, this is it," Kia said, running an anxious hand

through the deep red of her hair. "Everybody stay calm. Gerdi, no tricks. We want them to trust us."

Gerdi was too busy keeping his eyes on the dark shapes that moved slowly through the mist to bother with a reply.

"Kia," Ty hissed in warning. "Your side."

She looked, and there she saw one of the Koth Taraan moving through the twisted trunks and thick vines towards them. The others kept their distance, but this one was coming purposefully closer, gradually gaining definition as it approached. It walked awkwardly and heavily, pushing through the gloom until it stood before them, and there it stopped.

It was the first good look any of them had ever got at a Koth Taraan. It was at least ten feet high, and probably six feet broad, plated from head to toe with thick, lumpy armour of a dark green hue. Its enormous shoulders dwarfed the small head that was set low between them. Its face was a broad, angular shape without ears, nose or mouth, but instead dominated by two immense, teardrop-shaped eyes of the purest black. It was not the only evidence of the strange proportions in the creature's body shape. For though its torso and its upper legs and arms were small, it possessed massive forearms, plated in armour, that ended in a set of thick ivory claws over a foot long. Similarly, its lower legs were huge, terminating in a flat, elephantlike foot clad in the same lumpen hide as covered most of its body. It was as if a boulder had simply stood up and uncurled itself.

The black, alien eyes were unreadable, but for Kia they reminded her uncomfortably of the cruel gaze of the Keriags, and she thought of what Taacqan had said to Ty just before he died, linking the two species somehow.

Nobody spoke. They were waiting to see what the creature would do. For a long time, it did not stir, except for moving its eyes from one of the Parakkans to the other, an action that was only visible by the sliding of the moist glint of light on its lenses.

It did not speak, or make a sound. Silently, it watched them.

Peliqua began to fidget nervously, glancing occasionally around to see if the others had moved closer.

"Say something, Kia," she urged quietly.

Kia swallowed. Now that she faced one of the creatures, she had no idea what she had intended to say to them. After a moment, she blinked sweat out of her eyes and spoke.

"We're not here to fight," she said through a dry

throat. "We're not trying to invade your territory. We just want to talk."

The creature turned its head slightly, so that it was looking at her. She felt her nerve failing under its gaze. Still it did not make a noise.

"Uh, Kia, you might want to see this," said Gerdi from behind her. She took a wary step back from the creature and looked where he was pointing. The Koth Taraan behind them were moving, ambling slowly aside to create a gap in the circle that surrounded them.

"They did that before!" Peliqua said. "It means they want us to go, I think."

An expression of fleeting anger crossed Kia's face. Ty laid a hand on her shoulder, and she composed herself again at his touch. Turning back to the creature that waited near them, she planted her staff hard into the ground in a gesture that meant they weren't going anywhere.

"No," she said levelly. "We've come this far, and we're not turning back now. We ask for an audience with you, with your leaders if you have them. We have important things we must discuss. Things that could affect the lives of both our races."

Ty looked from Kia's face to the creatures. Was she really getting through? he thought. Or was she just wasting her time, trying to communicate with something that was incapable of understanding her? And even if it could, how would it reply? They had no mouths, and their enormous claws were hardly suited to hand-signals.

The creature did not move or respond, just watched her with its alien eyes.

"I know you can understand me," Kia said stridently. "So listen to this. We have no desire to encroach on your land, but we are *not* leaving until we can talk to one of you about the matter that faces us all."

A long pause. And then, as one, the Koth Taraan that surrounded them suddenly broke from their immobility, raising their claws and stamping the ground; and each of them emitted a high-pitched screech, something that was less heard than felt, which sawed at their brains and made the Parakkans want to clutch at their heads.

They did not understand exactly what was happening, but the general signals were clear enough. Anger. A challenge.

Attack.

"Scatter!" Kia cried as the Koth Taraan that stood closer to her swung a massive claw down at her. She whirled out of the way, lashing her staff at the creature's head; but it was too small a target, and too well-protected by the thick shoulder armour. Her blow cracked harmlessly into its hide.

The Parakkans broke and ran, knowing that there was no hope in a stand-up fight with these creatures. They were outnumbered, and the Koth Taraan were on home ground, as well as possessing a great physical advantage. Agility was the Parakkans' only asset, and so they split up to use the terrain to greatest effect. All except Ty, who stayed with Kia, his hooking-flail a deadly blur in his hands, and would not leave her side.

Vines lashed at Jaan's face and tangled in the thick ropes of his hair as he ran in search of decent defensive ground. All around him, the sounds of the lumbering Koth Taraan as they crashed through the undergrowth was in his ears. The earth squelched beneath his boots, threatening to give way at any moment, but something compelled him to keep going, zigzagging randomly in case he should —

"Duck!" bellowed a voice from in front of him, and suddenly he was face-to-face with Hochi, the big man's warhammer held ready for a swing. He threw himself to the mud, rolling aside as a claw the size of his upper torso carved a lethal path through the mist where he had just been, and its owner thundered out of the trees a moment later. But Hochi was ready for it, his weapon crashing into the Koth Taraan's back with a force that would have shattered most of the bones in a man's body.

The great creature staggered, stumbled . . . and then stood erect again, fixing Hochi with a black gaze of malice.

"Mauni's Eyes," he cursed under his breath in wonder, then shouted: "Run!" at Jaan before following his own advice.

Gerdi threw himself aside as a massive shape barged past him, smashing into a tree and blasting a splintered dent in its trunk large enough to make it slowly topple, accompanied by the angry hiss of leaves as it went and ending in a booming splash as it hit the waterlogged ground. He hadn't even bothered to draw his shortblade or unlatch his crossbow; he knew the former would be useless and the latter would take too much time to operate at such close quarters. He was vaguely aware of Peliqua nearby, her red braided hair coiling around her body as she dodged away from the clumsy, brutal strikes that swept at her from all directions. Her manriki-gusari was as ineffective as his own weapon, and she, like him, was forced into a desperate dance of evasion, praying that something would happen soon that would turn the tables of what looked like a hopeless situation.

Kia fought like a wildcat, but even she knew that their position was untenable. There were too many of them, and they were too well-armoured to damage in any noticeable way. They were slow, but they were everywhere, and the terrain beneath her feet seemed to collude with the enemy to trip her up and wrongfoot her, laying her open to a hit. And it would only take one hit . . .

The stones in her back burned with power that ached for release, glowing dark red, six blazing points along her spine. But she could not afford the concentration that creating and maintaining one of her golems would entail; and the Koth Taraan were barely giving her breathing space to release the Flow that writhed impatiently within her spirit-stone battery.

Even amid the chaos of the fight, she could not help thinking that if Ryushi were here, this could all be over in a moment. And even as adrenaline streamed through her system, and her long-honed reflexes carried her away from the jaws of death again and again, she still felt a stab of guilt and regret that they had not parted on better terms.

Sweat ran along Peliqua's grey skin as she threw herself out of the way of another blow, moving on instinct. She hit the ground in a roll and hopped to her feet in a half-crouch as the long, vicious claws slashed through the air inches above her head. Her muscles were beginning to ache now, and oh, she could have cried with frustration that she didn't have a set of spirit-stones right at this moment, like the Dominion-folk did. But she refused to despair; despair was not an emotion she was familiar with. There was always a way, always a solution.

And then she saw it.

She tugged at the manriki-gusari around her waist, and it came free. She backflipped out of a two-clawed smash, pulling the chain taut as she sailed through the murky air, and lashed out with it as her feet struck the turf. The lead-weighted tip shot out like a whip, cracking between her assailant's shoulder armour and its huge forearms to strike the side of its head, just at the edge of one of its wide eyes. It let out an ear-splitting screech, flinching backwards with its claws crossed in front of its face, and stumbled backwards in retreat.

"The eyes!" she shouted. "Go for their eyes!"

It was as if the Koth Taraan heard her words. For the briefest of seconds, they hesitated as one; and in that moment Kia had the time she needed to release the Flow. She sent herself into the earth, feeling the slip and slide of the mud, seizing it, engulfing every tiny molecule, pulling them, molding them, shaping them. The whole process took only a split second, but it was infinitely complex, a subtle play of forces on the most microscopic level. And the ground responded to her, suddenly reaching up with four great, brutal hands and clamping on to the arms and legs of the Koth Taraan that she faced, pulling it hard, toppling it backwards to the earth and pinning it there, spreadeagled.

But it was strong. She had never felt anything strain with so much power against the bonds that she maintained. So strong, in fact, that she couldn't hold it . . .

"Ty! The eyes! Kill it!" Jaan yelled, appearing from nowhere, his dagnas jabbing and darting as he attempted to hold off another one of the Koth Taraan.

Ty's hooking-flail spun in his hand, carving an edged circle in the dim light. But he did not strike. He looked at Kia with an expression of torment; but Kia was struggling to keep the creature held down, and could not help him. It fixed its dark eyes on him, endless pools of black in its inhuman face.

"Kill it!" Jaan cried.

Hochi roared as he slammed his warhammer into another Koth Taraan. His weapon was the only one which seemed to have any kind of effect at all on the massive things, and then it was only to stagger and stun them. Now he was flailing recklessly, battle-fired, putting his great weight into every swing in the hope that he could outmatch these creatures by brute force. But he was *too* reckless, and he was suddenly surprised by a swift step back by his opponent that caused his hammer to miss by inches. The overswing left him vulnerable, and he saw the terrible claws of the Koth Taraan sweeping up to open his chest; but at the last second, he released his grip on his hammer, and the shift in momentum lent him just enough inertia to throw himself out of the way. There was a feeble tearing noise as his thin, wet shirt was ripped open in three great strips and fell in shreds around him, but he escaped with only a long scratch along his belly. Escape was a relative term, however; for he landed on his bottom in the mud, weaponless, and suddenly there were two Koth Taraan looming over him, lunging in for the kill . . .

"I *can't*!" Ty shouted, letting his hooking-flail spin to a stop in his fist and hang limply over his knuckles. "I won't be a murderer again!"

It was something he had always feared, ever since his time in Os Dakar. Then, as the Pilot of the Bear Claw, he had been responsible for the deaths of many in the fight for his own survival. The experience had scarred him, left him with a lasting aversion to killing; and though he could cope with the deaths of monsters like the Jachyra and the Keriags at his hands, he could not murder what might be a sentient being, only defending its territory.

"They're *animals*!" Jaan fairly screamed. "*Kill* it!"

But by then it was too late, for at that moment Kia cried out and fell backwards as if pushed by an invisible force, and the Koth Taraan tore through its bonds and rose to its feet, massive and powerful again . . .

And they stopped.

The claws halted mere centimeters from Hochi's exposed chest, their vicious tips suddenly arrested. The attacks on the others suddenly diminished to nothing, the creatures stepping back and reverting to a ready stance, slightly crouched, their black eyes watchful. The Parakkans held their positions, breathing heavily, wary of this sudden reprieve.

Hochi did not dare move as the Koth Taraan's claw came closer, until it was scraping the hair off his chest, and gently, delicately lifted Tochaa's pendant on its sharp tip, bringing it closer to the creature's face. Then it let the pendant fall, and stood up, taking a step backwards.

The one who had first approached them, the one Kia had entrapped in the earth, tipped its head to the side in a gesture that none of them recognized; and a moment later, it spoke, though the words seemed to be coming from *inside* their ears rather than from outside.

((We will talk)) it said, and the Koth Taraan turned their backs and began to lumber away, leaving the bewildered Parakkans with no choice but to pick themselves up and follow.

8

Only the Spoils

Calica had had enough.

It seemed to her that there were two forces fighting within her, and both were to do with pride. She did not dare tell Ryushi how she felt about him, because she thought that rejection would destroy her; and yet she was disgusted with herself for not having the courage to face up to the task, and that emotion dented her self-image badly. For a long while, the former force had held sway over her; but the latter one had been steadily growing, gathering strength as she let her torment drag on longer and longer, until eventually it had overwhelmed her.

This is stupid, she told herself. Childish and stupid. You've come of age; Ryushi's almost done the same.

You're responsible enough to handle this, and he's responsible enough to take it. It's time to stop messing around and get on with it.

So now she strode across the grounds of Base Usido, her determination lending her a purposeful step, heading for Ryushi's hut. The endless activity around her held no interest; her thoughts were all trapped inside, whirling and fluttering like trapped fireflies in a jar. She felt nervous, and more than a little sick, but she would not allow herself to turn back now. Not now that she'd made up her mind.

She remembered how she and Ryushi had talked on the way back from their meeting with Whist. She'd hardly even been paying attention to the words that passed between them; her traitorous mind kept on turning to his quirky smile, his elfin features, his clear, confident eyes. That had been two cycles ago, but she still remembered how she had felt as he talked morosely about having to turn down Whist's deal. He was plainly cut up about it, having his hopes raised like that, but he knew that he could never trust Whist, and to do so would be tantamount to giving himself up to Aurin. But while she had made the appropriate sympathetic comments, she had not been thinking at all about what he had been saying. Instead, she had been warring with her own feelings, debating the moment when she would finally declare herself to him. Selfish, but then love *was* selfish. And besides, he had done a good enough job of persuading himself that Whist's offer was too dangerous without her helping him out.

But even if he had decided otherwise, she would have gone with him. She was just thankful that he had seen sense and decided not to return.

And so now the moment was here. She walked towards the cluster of huts, her feet seeming to get more reluctant with every step, and thought about what she would say. She had every word ready, hanging at the back of her throat in preparation . . . for it had to be perfect, if she was to carry this through without faltering. She went, as if in a dream, along the paths between the black wychwood huts, seeking his out. And when she found it, she paused for a long time before the door. It took the appearance of somebody further up the trail to spur her into action; after all, she couldn't be seen just standing aimlessly outside someone's home. She took a deep breath and knocked.

There was no reply.

A flood of relief washed through her, but it was followed quickly by a rolling mist of suspicion. She pushed gently on the door, and it creaked open.

"Ryushi?" she asked, stepping inside.

The hut was empty. His sword and pack were gone.

"Oh, you idiot," she said under her breath, closing her eyes and letting her head sink.

"You gotta admit," Whist said, "the guy did well for himself."

The province of Maar spread out before them, stretching to the horizon and beyond. Under the faint glare of the dark sun, it was beautiful. Fields — not square, like those of the Dominions, but elliptical, with a diamond-shaped central field for tessalation — stretched out across the flat land, sparkling softly with the fragile crystalline plants of Kirin Taq. There were orchards and vineyards, great strips of them; there were well-maintained roads winding between little clusters of buildings and farms; there was a smooth lake of the darkest blue, flashing shivers of dim light from its gently stirring surface. A trio of wyverns, flying in formation, scraped across the blue-purple sky, the red-armoured Riders on their backs bent low in their harnesses.

Ryushi took a step back, retreating into the shadow of the trees, watching the airborne beasts warily. They were standing on the provincial border, at the edge of a wychwood forest that fringed a low hill. The borders between the provinces were defined by features of geography rather than barriers with guards; after all, strife between the thanes was nonexistent under Aurin's rule. They were little more than caretakers of her land, and if any of them should get ideas above their station, they had a habit of disappearing. . . .

It was an idyllic place, the province of Maar. But it had been bought with the blood of Ryushi's father, Banto, and the thane who ruled it was responsible for his murder. Ryushi looked over the land and saw only the spoils of Takami's betrayal.

Blink whuffed at Whist's feet, his head lying on his paws, his eyes lazily following the path of the distant wyvern patrol.

"Don't it strike you as strange, though?" Whist said, standing with his weight on one leg. "I mean, just that . . . just that *one single* incident has changed everything. He's a noble, with all this land. You and Kia are members of Parakka. And look where you are now. You're following a guy you plainly don't trust in order to kill your own brother." He smiled wryly. "And all this 'cause Takami decided to betray your family. If not for that, it might all still be as it was. Makes you think, huh? How fragile everything is, or something."

"I never had you pegged for philosophy, Whist,"

131

Ryushi commented dryly. "I thought backstabbing was more your line."

Blink gave a warning growl in the back of his throat, but Whist just smiled. "Just remember, smart guy, I'm the only one who can get you to Takami. A deal's a deal, so why don't we just pretend to like each other for the moment?"

"Okay, I can do that," Ryushi replied. "So what's the next move, anyway?"

"First trick is to get across the province. We've been travelling along the borders the last couple of days; it's easy to stay out of sight that way. But Takami's stronghold is right in the center of Maar, and both of us Dominion guys are gonna stand out in a land full of Kirins."

"I assume you've got a plan," Ryushi said.

"Natch," he said. "Follow me."

They made their way along the edge of the forest, keeping hidden among the thinning periphery of trees. They travelled in this manner for a short while, until they had moved around the curve of the hill and could see a little more of the landscape of Maar.

"Down there," Whist said.

Ryushi had seen the building several minutes beforehand, but he had not attached any special importance to it. Now that his attention was directed that way, however, he looked more closely. It was a strange shape, like two horseshoes back-to-back and joined in the center, made of thick panels of weathered and beaten metal that looked faintly blue in the twilight. The body of the building was curved and rounded; tapering towards the four horns of the horseshoe-shapes, and a wide road ran through the center of it, coming from the neighboring province and heading away between the fields.

"What is it?"

"It's a land-train depot," Whist replied. "You've never seen one before?"

"Guess not," Ryushi said. "So what's it do?"

Whist absently ran a hand over his dog's back as he spoke. "You might have seen land-trains around in the Dominions, right?"

"From a distance," Ryushi said, remembering the battle at the Ley Warren.

"Well, anyway," came the reply, "they didn't have any of this stuff in Kirin Taq until Macaan started getting Machinists over to build them. They're great big heavy things, and it takes a lot of kick to make 'em go. So every so often they have to stop at depots to get the energy back up. See, land-trains are one of the only vehicles that you don't need a Pilot like Ty to drive; they've got engines. But you know what it's like; even the Machinists can't make engines that work without making them enormous. Plus they need drop-off points to unload and load cargo. So that's why they have those depots."

"We're gonna stow on a land-train?"

"Sure," Whist grinned. "If we get the right one, it'll take us all the way across the province. And right into Takami's stronghold."

"What, you think he won't have measures to stop that happening?" Ryushi said skeptically. "Otherwise anyone could just wander into his palace."

"Of course he does," Whist replied. "But I've worked for him, remember? There are ways and means. Unfortunately," he said, scratching his arm beneath his heavy glove, "it still don't mean it's gonna be *easy*, exactly." He looked at Ryushi, a glimmer in his eye. "But then it wouldn't be any fun, now would it?"

Ryushi didn't reply, his eyes fixed on the depot below. After a moment, Whist sighed at his lack of response, and then muttered: "Let's get going then," before leading the way down the hill, Blink padding after him.

Though the hill was quite exposed and devoid of cover, the lack of light and the sparseness of the nearby population worked for them. Even though Kirin eyes had long since adapted to the low level of brightness from the corona of the sun, most of the settlements had been built some way in from the provincial border, and the intruders would be little more than specks to the people in the nearest village as they ran low and swift down the hillside. Still, Ryushi kept his eyes out in case the Riders on wyvern-back might return.

The depot did not appear to be guarded on the outside. As they neared, they saw only the curved iron shell of the exterior, and the only sign of life was the faint huffing and clanking that came from within. The road was deserted in either direction, except for a distant group of pakpak riders that were heading into the province.

"I don't like this," he said. "It's too easy. There should be guards."

"Why waste the guards when a trespasser can't get *in*?" Whist strolled boldly up to the side of the depot, which towered many times his height, and rapped it with a knuckle. The sound fell dead. "Solid. A foot thick. Nothing's getting through there." He paused, then raised an eyebrow as he looked Ryushi over. "Well, actually *you* could, if your little trick back on Os Dakar was anything to go by."

Ryushi shrugged. He remembered well the moment

when he had been forced to unleash his power to annihilate the Keriags a few moments before their escape. "It wouldn't do any good, though. It'd make so much noise, they'd be bound to come and find me."

"And by then you'd be too weak to fight," Whist finished.

Ryushi looked at him strangely. He hadn't been about to reveal that particular facet of his power. "You know an awful lot about me and my family, Whist," he commented in a tone that suggested he found it unpleasant.

Whist beamed. "It's all one-sided. Very negative. Takami told me most of it; the rest I picked up from gossip in the stronghold. Correct me if I'm wrong," he winked, "but I think Tak's still sore you aced him in the Ley Warren."

"He's gonna be a lot sorer when I kill him," Ryushi said.

Whist made a face, conceding him the point. "Well, yeah, I s'pose so," he replied. "Anyway, do we wanna get in here or don't we?"

"Guess," Ryushi replied sarcastically.

"That's the spirit!" Whist said, full of spurious enthusiasm. "Now where'd that dog of mine get to?"

"Like you don't know," Ryushi said, as Blink nuzzled

Whist's thigh, whining as if to say: *I'm here, look, it's me!*

"Oh, right," he said, dropping to one knee and rubbing Blink's face between his palms. "Think you can pull off some of your magic for us, big guy?"

Blink barked excitedly. Whist hushed him, and the dog calmed down a little; then he beckoned Ryushi over. "See," he said. "After I found Blink could do it once, I started experimenting a little. Turns out he can wink all kinds of stuff with him when he goes. Put your arm around him and hug yourself as close as you can."

Ryushi hesitated for a second, reluctance on his face, and then did as he was instructed. Whist did the same, holding on to the body of the huge dog as if he were a barrel and they were trying to keep afloat. Up close, Blink smelled overpoweringly musty, and Ryushi wrinkled his nose.

"Are we gonna wink onto a land-train?" Ryushi asked. His experiences of being shifted between the worlds by Elani had left him a little wary of allowing himself to be transported by someone else. Especially a dog.

"'Fraid not," Whist replied apologetically. "He's got to be reasonably confident of where he's going, or he

137

won't make the jump. He could wink himself half into the floor or something. But he's got kind of an instinct for short hops; and this *is* just a short hop. From *this* side of the wall . . ." he put his palm against the metal of the depot wall ". . . to *that* one. Now hold on."

The dog blinked, and Ryushi felt a jolt in his body that made all his muscles jump simultaneously, a split-second of nothingness, and then their surroundings flicked from the cool air of Kirin Taq to the grinding, roaring interior of the depot.

They disengaged themselves from the body of Blink, and Whist made a fuss of him while Ryushi's brain tried to catch up with his senses. They were on a narrow gantry, buried behind a bank of black, steaming machines. Imported Dominion glowstones provided a dim orange light, and the air smelled acrid, and felt strangely greasy in a way that Ryushi couldn't define. All around them was the deafening noise of gears clashing, pistons pumping, and the hiss of hot steam; but at least they had not appeared in front of a guard, and they were in one piece.

"Where to now?" Ryushi asked, sliding his sword free.

"What, *I* should know?" Whist asked exasperatedly.

"Let's just look around. It's not like we're gonna miss something as big as a land-train, now is it?"

"I thought you had a *plan*," Ryushi replied. "When I hear the word *plan*, I take it to mean more than just a vague idea of the direction we're meant to be going in."

"Yeah, but when I have a plan it *works*," Whist said, standing up again, his shoes clanking on the metal grills beneath their feet. "You can moan at me after we've been caught. Until then, shut *up*; you're beginning to tick me off."

Ryushi swallowed back a retort. Arguing wouldn't do them any good here. Especially as Whist and Blink were his only way out of the depot at the moment.

"Okay, let's go," he said.

They crept through the bellowing guts of the depot, moving carefully along the maze of gantries that ran between the huge machines. They were not worried about the sound of their footsteps being heard over the din, but as they did not know the layout of the place, they were aware that they might run into guards at any moment; and if the alarm was raised, the game was up. So they peered warily around every corner, and jumped at every unexpected clank or jet of steam. Whist sent Blink ahead to scout out routes, his mind riding behind the

139

dog's eyes as it slunk through the depot, sharing its vision. Occasionally, they saw the black form of a Guardsman wandering disinterestedly along a nearby gantry, and had to backtrack to go around him. Once, they were nearly surprised by a sentry who appeared from the top of a narrow set of stairs; but they managed to hide before he saw them. It was tense, but they were making steady progress, and the depot was not heavily guarded.

At one point, while they were taking a short rest in the shelter of a pair of huge, hissing pipes, Ryushi asked Whist what all the machinery was for.

"The fuel," he replied, having to shout to be heard over the racket of the pipes. "All this set-up is just for the fuel to make the land-trains run. You think it's easy to extract all that stuff from the earth, or to ship it to the depots? Nah, they just do it all here. But it's such a massive job, it's hardly worth it." He picked at a piece of metal flash on the grill at his feet. "If man was meant to drive, he wouldn't have been given spirit-stones, right? I think they keep these land-trains going more to keep the Pilot's Guild nervous, y'know? Like, 'we can do this without you,' or something. Besides, it's hard to get Pilots over in Kirin Taq. Since they made having spirit-stones an execution offense — except for the nobles and their armies and so on — the supply of Pilots sorta dried up."

"You *are* well-informed," Ryushi said, exaggeratedly impressed.

"I keep my ear to the ground," Whist replied, missing the irony in Ryushi's voice because of the noise that surrounded them.

Their encounters with the Guardsmen became more and more frequent as they headed towards what they thought was the center of the building, where the two horseshoe-shapes joined up and a tunnel ran through them. Whist assured Ryushi that this was where the land-trains were resupplied, but he was not sure of the exact route to get to it. Ryushi guessed that they were not far off, though, because avoiding the sentries had by now become less of a nuisance and more of a full-time occupation. He wished Gerdi were here now. The green-haired Noman boy's ability to alter his appearance would have been invaluable. But this was *his* problem, and he could not allow anyone else to be endangered by it. And that included Calica.

"Alright! Am I not the *best*?" Whist suddenly said next to him. Ryushi blinked in momentary disorientation and then said: "What?"

"We're here," Whist grinned.

Ryushi glanced around. They were on a gantry like any other, still penned in by machinery. Blink was away somewhere out of sight.

"No, we're not," said Ryushi in puzzlement. "And where's *here*, anyway?"

"The land-train, you — " Whist began to snap, and then caught himself. "Oh, right. Sorry. Blink's found the land-train. It's just around the next corner."

Ryushi gave him an odd look. Riding behind Blink's eyes, Whist had forgotten where his real body was. Sometimes, his relationship with his dog was a little *too* close.

They turned a right-angle, and there they found Blink waiting for them, sitting on his haunches, his tongue lolling happily. Before them, there was a long railing that ran along the side of the gantry; and beyond that, there was the awesome spectacle of the land-train.

From where they stood, high up in the arch of the massive tunnel that ran through the center of the depot, it crouched beneath them like a giant, fat spider. Eight enormous wheels on sprung axles supported the lozenge-shaped central body that hid between them, four on each side. The wheels were thick and bulky, adapted to protect the vehicle from shocks as it sped over the terrain, and each one was heavily rutted and grooved for grip. The body of the vehicle was smooth, with a rounded front and back end, and a curved strip of dark Dominion glass for the cockpit. A loading-ramp was just visible between the wheels, lowered from the vehicle's underbelly; large-bore pipes ran from the vast iron fuel tanks of the depot to intakes on the land-train's flanks.

"Come on," said Whist. "Just need to get close enough, and Blink'll get us in."

Tiny insects against the enormous labyrinth of gantries and ladders and stairs that sprawled over the sides of the tunnel, they began to make their way downwards. As they descended through the many levels of grinding, roaring noise, the land-train seemed to rise higher and higher, until finally it dwarfed them entirely beneath its massive wheels and ironbound hide. They had a few more near-misses with sentries, but they were nothing worse than what they had already gone through. After a short while, as they hurried along another metal walkway, Ryushi said what had been bothering him for some time.

"This is too easy," he remarked.

"What, because we haven't been caught yet? Are you *never* happy?" Whist cried over the din. "Look, they don't keep a heavy guard inside because nobody can get *in*. They guard the tunnel mouth at either end *very* carefully, if that makes you feel any better, but — "

"Hey!" came a cry from behind them, and they whirled to see two Guardsmen running towards them, their black armour sheening orange in the glowstone light, their halberds held with the force-muzzles levelled at the intruders.

"Ah, now you've jinxed us," Whist complained, and his gloved hand flashed out from his belt, two razor-edged discs spinning through the air from his outstretched palm faster than the eye could follow. The Guardsmen jerked as the discs hit; one was taken in the throat, in the narrow gap between his faceplate and his chest protector, while the other got the disc through the eyepiece. They toppled in a clatter of armour and were still.

Whist looked back at Ryushi. "Satisfied?"

Ryushi didn't rise to the goad. Instead, he said: "Are we close enough yet for your dog to get us in?"

"He thinks so," Whist replied immediately.

"Then let's hide those bodies and get on board," Ryushi said, his tone rigidly efficient and businesslike to mask his reaction to Whist's casual slaughter of the Guardsmen. He'd been forced to kill before, and he'd kill again, of that he was sure; but if he ever got so blasé about it that it ceased to affect him, he didn't think he could live with himself. Sometimes he even thought he understood Ty's problem with the subject. Maybe his friend feared he would become like Whist was; a creature with no morals, for whom the killing of a man was merely the removal of an annoying obstacle.

But there was one man whose death would bring Ryushi no remorse, and it was that face that filled his mind as he and Whist set to work.

9

A Pantheon of Dim Ghosts

If Kia and the others had been footsore and tired before, then they were on the verge of dropping from exhaustion by the time they reached the Koth Taraan's settlement. They had been travelling for some time before they had even encountered the huge creatures, and the subsequent fight had drained them further. But when the strange truce had been called — and they still had no clear idea *why* the Koth Taraan had stopped attacking — they had been forced to follow their departing adversaries or be left behind. After going through everything that they had, Kia was not about to let the promise of a meeting get away from her; but the creatures did not seem to tire, and the wet ground sucked at their boots and made each step twice as hard as it should have been. They struggled to negotiate shallow bogs that the Koth Taraan swept effortlessly through; they fought to untangle themselves from the annoyingly adhesive vines that draped across their path; they clambered over the curling, stone-hard roots of the marsh trees.

In this manner, they continued for perhaps another tenth-cycle, their heads light and their limbs heavy but unable to stop for fear of losing their guides, who seemed almost oblivious to their presence. Gerdi collapsed at one point, but the barechested Hochi picked up the young Noman boy and carried him on his broad back; his oxlike endurance was standing him in good stead compared to the rest of them. Peliqua was flagging badly, too, but she never made even the slightest complaint. Despite her scatty manner, Peliqua was one of Parakka's most reliable members, and she had a core of steel.

And then suddenly they emerged at the shore of a vast, shallow lake of brackish, weed-choked water, and there was the settlement. It was built on the many islands that lay just above the murky surface, linked together by simple, flat bridges of some kind of artificially made mud ceramic. The same substance had been used in the construction of their dwellings; tall, wide igloos of a light, sandy brown that were stacked together in clusters, built in mounds with each spherical facet merging into the next, like a pile of snowballs. Circular holes, twelve feet or so in diameter, pocked the surface of each cluster, and from within came a warm red-yellow glow. Torches on poles surrounded the islands, standing alone in the lake, throwing a hazy illumination through the marsh-mist. Overhead, the trees had grown close, and nothing of the sky could be seen. It was an enclosed world, an island of islands in the marsh; and as Kia saw it, she managed a weak smile of triumph.

Dwellings. Speech. The Koth Taraan were not mindless things; they were a *people.*

One of the creatures that had been guiding them — it *could* have been the one that spoke, but Kia wasn't sure — suddenly half-turned and looked at them, as if to see if they were still there. And then its voice rang in their heads again, seeming to emanate from within their skulls rather than entering through their ears.

((Stay here. Sleep. We will return))

Kia nodded. The creature did not seem to know what to make of that, so she affirmed her agreement vocally. With no further word, the Koth Taraan made their way across one of the bridges to the settlement, leaving the Parakkans to collapse in the wet mud in exhaustion.

"I'll watch out for us," said Hochi stolidly, pulling on

a new shirt to replace his ripped one and settling himself in a cross-legged position with his hammer across his lap.

Soaked, mud-smeared, and bone-tired, the others wearily dragged out their blankets, and fell asleep the moment they hit horizontal.

Even in the marsh, there were Glimmer plants growing in sparse clusters, little dots of light that speckled the darkness. When Jaan opened his eyes, the patch that he saw amid the drooping leaves and vines told him that they had been out for a full cycle; the color was almost exactly what it had been when they fell asleep. He rubbed the thick ropes of his hair muzzily, his palm running over the small ornaments and beads that resided there. Rummaging through his pack, he dug out a wineskin full of sugary juice. Taking a swig, he noted with a smile that Hochi had fallen asleep in his cross-legged position and was gently snoring. He put the skin back in his pack and got out of his blanket, stood up and stretched his aching spine, turned around and jumped half out of his senses.

A Koth Taraan was there, motionless, next to where the others were sleeping. It was standing in the neutral stance that the creatures seemed to adopt whenever they were still, with its massive forearms slightly crossed in front of it and its armoured back bent forward a little, as if it were leaning towards something just ahead. It was watching him with its wide, black eyes.

((You are different from the others)) came its voice inside his head, and strangely it carried with it the smudged impression of the color purple, seeming to stain the message as it passed through Jaan's mind.

He didn't know what surprised him more; the appearance of the creature or the fact that it was *speaking* to him. He scrambled for a reply.

"Uhhh . . .how do you mean?"

((Kirins. Dominion-folk. But you are neither)) Again, the purple cloud of watercolor attended the words, but this time it was more distinct. Confusion.

"I'm a halfbreed," Jaan said, and even through his surprise a little bitterness leaked into his voice.

((But which culture do you choose?))

"Neither want me," Jaan replied, his yellow-irised eyes looking into the black of the Koth Taraan's. "So I choose my own."

((You are different from the others)) the creature repeated.

"No," Jaan said. "We're all the same. We just look different."

A warm flooding of reddish-yellow washed through his mind. Approval.

((Who are you?)) it said.

"I'm Jaan," he replied.

((Who are you?)) came the question again. This time, though he couldn't have said how, Jaan realized that the question was meant to encompass all of them.

"Parakka," he said.

The creature was silent for a few seconds. Then: *((Wake Parakka. You will come soon))* And with that pronouncement, it turned and lumbered away, back to the settlement.

Jaan stood where he was for a moment, watching the huge form as it departed with slow, deliberate steps. He didn't know what to make of the exchange that had just taken place, or of what the creature had intended to divine from it. Puzzled and a little shaken, he woke the others, beginning with Hochi so that the big man could avoid the ribbing he'd get from Gerdi about nodding off on watch. They grumbled as they forced themselves awake, but when Jaan told them what had happened they were fascinated, and there was a frantic round of suggestions as they tried to guess what his encounter had meant. They were still nowhere near a conclusion when Ty pointed out that the Koth Taraan were coming, and they gathered up the remainder of their soiled blankets and bedding and packed them away, then stood ready to meet the entourage, as proudly as they could manage considering that they were covered head-to-toe in dirt and grime.

There were five of them who approached across the mist-shrouded bridge. Jaan looked for the one who had talked to him before, but it was near impossible to tell the creatures apart.

((Come with us)) said one of them; but which one, they could not have said.

They obeyed, accompanying the Koth Taraan on their unhurried return across the simple, unadorned bridge to the settlement. The curious stacks of spherical ceramic igloos had their highest points obscured by the mist — which had thickened as they had slept — but the lights of their circular entrances still shone, looking like hazy, disembodied suns in the white gloom.

They passed within the ring of torches that stood in the gently stirring swamp-water and onto the first island. Kia had originally thought that was the igloo-cluster that they were heading for, but they were led around that to one of the smaller satellite islands that formed a junction between three others, linked by the flat bridges, and onto another one near the center of the lake. This one was the largest by far, with an enormous mountain of igloos, surrounded by a jumble of smaller heaps at its wide base. One of the glowing openings lay near ground level, and it was here that they were taken, stepping into the welcoming light.

Kia caught her breath. If she had ever had any doubts about her determination that the Koth Taraan were not just beasts, they were swept away as she stepped into the settlement. The interior of the large igloo that they had entered had an intricacy that belied the simple exterior. From the circular entrance, two sweeping ramps curved away on either side, meeting further up the igloo in a platform and crossing over again. Similar curved and sloping walkways wound their way up towards exits, high up the walls of the igloo. Kia's first impression was to think of the Snapper Run that she and Gerdi had endured on Os Dakar, but that was only partially accurate. The Snapper Run had been rough and chaotic in its construction, and held up by ugly pillars. The architecture of this place was perfectly symmetrical, and despite its many layers it was easy on the eye. Also, rather than pillars, the walkways were banked up with solid matter, so that the "floor" of the igloo seemed to slope diagonally up and away from them.

But the walkways and ramps in themselves were

nothing. What pulled Kia up short was the decoration. Directly in front of them, between the two curving ramps on either side, was an enormous wooden sculpture, forty feet high or more, a smooth shape that twisted and dived inward on itself before shattering into a core of jagged spikes. Its surface was carved with a multitude of tiny black symbols on the creamy wood, thicker at some points and sparser at others, to draw the attention of the observer to certain parts of the shape. Higher up the cavern, the greenish swamp-water poured through an ornamental outlet and into a series of trenches that ran down the sloped interior, sometimes breaking up into terrifically intricate patterns, grids and spirals and other shapes that Kia's brain could barely grasp. She didn't understand the meaning of what she saw; it came from alien minds, incomprehensible to her. But what it said about the Koth Taraan as a people was far more important.

"Wow," Peliqua said, looking up at the sculpture. A moment later, she added: "I don't get it. What *is* it?"

Jaan punched her gently in the ribs to remind her about her lack of manners.

"Oh, right, sorry," she said, after a few moments' confusion as to why her brother had assaulted her.

They were led through several more chambers, each one populated by a few dozen Koth Taraan, engaged in unfathomable activities or resting in their neutral stance. Occasionally they saw one of the creatures intent on the creation of another sculpture, or on the construction of a new part of an igloo. These ones wore thick metal rings around the tips of their long claws, each ring bearing a different-shaped tool for their work; hooks, serrated edges, devices for smoothing texture, all controlled with a delicacy that seemed at odds with their vicious, unwieldly digits. The Parakkans watched in wonder the civilization that they had stumbled upon.

Eventually the Koth Taraan halted outside a semicircular entrance to a new chamber, from which fingers of swamp-mist — which had been absent inside the rest of the igloos — curled out teasingly.

((The Koth Macquai is inside)) said one of their escorts. *((If you try to harm Koth Macquai, we will first kill you and then destroy one of your human villages for each of the limbs we tear from your bodies))*

The message was delivered with a thick black hue, emphasizing the threat. Jaan frowned. Why was it that they only got the colors sometimes, and at other times they didn't?

"We're here on a mission of *peace*," Kia said firmly, with admirable courage in the face of such creatures. "We don't want to hurt anyone."

The escorts stepped aside wordlessly, allowing them entrance to the chamber. Glancing warily at their huge hosts, they went inside.

The mist shrouded them immediately, yet strangely it was not cold as it had been outside but stiflingly warm. The floor of this chamber was covered with irregularly ɹaped pools of marshy water, a reddish glow from the bottom of each underlighting the gently swaying weeds. The mist seemed to emanate from the surface of these pools, lapping across the floor and rising in swirls and eddies.

They forged forward through the layers of obscuring warmth that filled the chamber, following Kia's lead as she picked her way between the pools along the rough, grainy floor. It was a small cavern by comparison to the others, for it took them only a short while before they reached the other side, and came into the presence of the Koth Macquai.

First the shadow of the creature had begun to form out of the mist, an indefinable blackness within the white, and then the curtains of vapor had seemed to tear aside and they saw it, standing in a cavern alcove in the wall, an arch surrounded by a multitude of carvings and inscriptions. A pair of torches blazed on either side. The Koth Macquai was like its kin, the Koth Taraan, but its natural armour had branched out around it like a stag's antlers, curving into horny ridges and plates. Its shoulder armour had become almost grotesquely ornate; its back had sprouted fingers of hide like a combination of a headdress and rigid wings. Its elbows and knees bristled with a protrusion of thick, blunt spines. It was as if the armour had overgrown the creature inside it; for Kia, even in her awe, could not see how it could possibly move and fight as a normal Koth Taraan did.

Then she realized; it was not a freak of the race, nor a separate thing from the other Koth Taraan. It was merely *old*. Perhaps the creatures' armour continued growing throughout their lives. She wished that she had seen some of their young to back up her theory, but there had been none in evidence as they travelled through the cluster, or she hadn't recognized them if there had been.

The Koth Macquai raised its tiny head within the massive frame of its body and looked at them. Hochi dropped to one knee and bowed his head, and the others, seeing him, followed suit.

((We have no such customs here)) the voice came inside their head, like a warm autumn breeze. *((But I thank you for your display of respect. Please rise))*

They stood, facing once more the ancient alien being, and waited for it to speak again.

((Forgive the attitude of the elder Brethren)) the Koth Macquai said. *((They begrudge your presence. We are not fond of strangers))*

"I understand," Kia said.

((Yet you interest me)) the creature continued. *((Where is the root of this determination to speak with us, even after we proved hostile?))*

"Desperation," Kia admitted honestly. "We have little hope, and turning back empty-handed would do us no good."

((Please explain)) came the response, and so she did. She told the Koth Macquai all about Parakka and the Dominions, Aurin and the Keriags, the Integration and the sudden change in their fortunes that had led to time becoming suddenly short for them. She had no reason to hide anything from it; they could not afford the luxury of dishonesty, and besides, she had a suspicion that the Koth Macquai would see through it anyway. She withheld only information that was unnecessary for the creature to know; locations of bases, numbers, and so on. It

was difficult to tell how much of what she was saying was information that the Koth Macquai already knew, but she went on anyway.

"If Parakka is wiped out," she concluded, "then the people of *both* worlds have no hope. Macaan's stranglehold gets tighter and tighter in the Dominions; it is already so tight here that this branch of Parakka could not have formed if we had not brought some of it with us from home. Soon, it will be over, unless we can develop some way to fight back."

((Your plight is not without merit)) said the creature, stirring its bulk slightly. *((But what do you want with us?))*

"We met a man who wanted to join Parakka. His name was Taacqan," Kia said. She waited for a reaction, but there was none that she could see. "He said he studied you, but I believe he *met* you, as we are doing now. He told us that you were a savage race of beasts, but I suspect he was trying to protect you. You value your solitude, I see that. But — "

((Where is Taacqan?)) the Koth Macquai interrupted.

"He died," Kia replied. "He was killed by Macaan's secret police for treason."

The others were silent. They had all unconsciously retreated a little, aware that this was Kia's show; now they watched the creature to see how it would respond to her news.

((Taacqan was a friend to us)) it said at length. *((Like you, he would not be turned away. He brought us news from beyond our lands, and sought to learn all he could about our people. He had the mind of an ambassador and the heart of a scholar. He, like you, warned us about Macaan. But though many protested against a human in our midst, as many were intrigued and alarmed by the stories he brought to us, he started a change, a stirring among the younger and more impetuous of the Brethren))*

Kia expected it to go on, to elaborate; but the Koth Macquai seemed to falter, uncertain whether it should continue. Then it changed the subject instead, cheating her.

((The elder Brethren feared this)) it said suddenly, its words riding on a grey tide of despondency. *((That if we allowed one of you into our territory, more would follow))*

Again, a silence.

((Tell me what you ask of us))

"A year ago, one of our operatives managed to read the thoughts of Macaan. She told us that he has an overriding desire to conquer anything and everything; it's a reaction against his fear of death by the disease that killed his parents and his Queen." Kia paused for a moment, took a breath, and continued. "I'm telling you this because I believe that your people will not be safe once Macaan has the Dominions under his power. Perhaps he hasn't come here before because his mind has been on the greater prizes, but he *will*, in the end."

((You come to warn us?))

"No," Kia said, her green eyes earnest. "I come to ask for your help. The power of Macaan's family is largely maintained by the Keriags. We have nothing that can fight them effectively. We need . . . *something*. Something we can use against them. And we came here in the hope that you could help us in some way, because if we don't get that something soon, it's all gonna be over."

Mentally, she cursed her inability to find the right words to say to this creature. She was no diplomat; Calica had the talent for that, not her. She was only honest. And even though these creatures did not appear to stand on ceremony, she was not sure that it would be enough.

((Your intentions are vague at best)) the Koth Macquai observed.

"So are our plans," Kia said. "We have nothing to

fight with, nothing that can bring the Keriags down. There are too many of them, and they are too strong. We have no defense. That is why we have to attack."

((It would seem)) the creature mused *((that your best course of action would be to determine the power that Aurin has over the Keriags, and destroy that power. That would solve your problems in one strike))*

"We've tried," Kia replied. "The Jachyra have rooted out every spy we've sent. We can't get close to her; and until we do, we can't learn about her. She and her father are so surrounded in legends and falsehoods, we can't hope to learn the truth from out here." She paused, and then dared to ask: "Do *you* know anything of the Keriags?"

((We know something of them)) the Koth Macquai said slowly, the words tinged with the murky blue of distaste. It shifted its weight slightly amid the swirling heat of the mists and then raised its unwieldly bulk from its alcove. *((Come with me))* it said, and they moved away a little as it stepped down from where it had been resting, the horny protrusions of its body clacking against each other. Slowly, the huge creature lumbered past them, heading into the white murk, and the Parakkans followed uncertainly, at a distance. It seemed like only a

short way before the Koth Macquai stopped in front of a wall, but the mists made it impossible to guage the size of the chamber, and Kia was completely disorientated. All that was forgotten, though, as her eyes fell on what the Koth Macquai was showing them.

It was a recording-wall. Kia had been told of them during her childhood by her Aunt Susa. They had once been common in the Dominions; remnants of past history, from before the time when paper was invented. Macaan had most of them destroyed soon after he came to power. But those had been merely carvings, etched into stone to depict events of great historical importance. This, on the other hand, was different. It was made of water.

The recording-wall was perhaps thirty feet high before it joined the curve of the outer sphere of the ceramic igloo, but from side to side its length was inestimable, disappearing into the haze in either direction. It was slightly sloped, with the top leaning back further than the bottom, and its surface was a maze of pictograms and icons, interspersed with pictures of things that Kia could not begin to guess at. The whole complex, intertwined network was composed of tiny, shallow trenches and sluices, and running along the top was a narrow stone trough of water that streamed down through the trenches into a gutter at floor level.

The detail was incredible. Junctions would suddenly pinch or expand to control the flow of water through a trench, thickening an outline with a gush or lending shading to a shape by gradiating less and less liquid to a series of lines. One pictogram would meld effortlessly into another without losing its own distinction. And the whole wall seemed to move, the tiny sparkle of the liquid making the figures shimmer in the mist, a pantheon of dim ghosts.

((Our history)) the Koth Macquai said. *((This is but a small part. There are many recording-walls. But they are purely an indulgence; we do not need them. We are an ancient folk, and our memory is eternal))*

Kia wondered what it meant by that; it was certainly a strange thing to say. But before she could ask, the Koth Macquai began to answer her previous question at last.

((The Koth Taraan and the Keriags shared a common ancester once, a long time ago, before humanity began. Many ages passed, and our two races grew apart. Each recognized itself in the other, and did not like what it saw. That is the beginning of many wars, Dominion child; and it was the beginning of ours, too))

It raised one huge claw, ridged and heavy, to indicate a section of the recording-wall where the pictures and pictograms seemed to take on an ugly, frenzied quality; and though they could not understand the language or decipher the meaning of the pictures, the Parakkans got the intended impression. *((Our war lasted for many of your lifetimes. But the Keriags were more numerous than we, for we have always been slow to breed as a race; and over time, they began to dominate. We retreated to the wetlands, which were unsuitable for the Keriags' biology. They were content to let us do so. Our people were beaten and chastened, but it was the price to be paid for giving in to our savage instincts. Our lesson had been learned. We will not war again on the Keriags, or any other race))*

"Not even for your own protection?" Hochi asked suddenly. "Not even to prevent Macaan invading your lands?"

((We will not make war simply to eliminate something that may or may not become a threat to us. We fight only to protect our territory. For the elder Brethren to allow strangers to our settlement is rarer than you will ever know. Your lives were spared by the courage of this one)) Here it turned its black eyes on Ty.

165

((Your pacifism, even in the face of death, gave the Brethren reason to pause. It interested them, and me. So I let you live))

"How could you have known when you weren't there?" Peliqua blurted.

((We have our ways, Kirin child, much as the Keriags do)) It shifted its gaze suddenly, placing it ponderously on Hochi. *((But there was something else that interested me. Your pendant))*

"You know what it *means*?" Hochi asked, his eyes alight with sudden hope.

A rainbow of colors flashed through their minds; the laughter of the Koth Taraan. *((Does that mean that you do not? How did you come about such an object?))*

So Hochi told it, his voice low with the pain of the memory, about the death of Tochaa in the Ley Warren, and how he had been given the pendant as the Kirin died.

"Now tell me, please . . . what does it mean?" he begged, taking it from his neck and holding it in the mud-smeared palm of his hand.

((It is a symbol from long ago, when the Kirin race was in its infancy. It is a piece of a language forgotten by humanity. That pendant is old, Dominion child, very old)) The creature paused, the seconds dragging by un-

bearably for Hochi. *((It represents a phrase taken from part of an old Kirin folktale. They believed that Kirin Taq and the Dominions were once one world, and that they were torn apart in a cataclysm they called the Sundering. To be literal, the symbol means division with the eventual hope of unity))* The creature seemed to creak as it leaned closer, its alien eyes fixed on Hochi's.

((In your language, it translates as Broken Sky))

About the Author

Chris Wooding was born in Leicester, England, in 1977. Besides *Broken Sky*, he is the author of *Kerosene, Crashing*, and *Endgame*, among others. He is a devout believer in bad horror movies, Anime videos, and the power of coffee.